THIS SPECIAL SIGNED EDITION OF

WAKING IN WINTER

**IS LIMITED TO 100 COPIES.
AN UNSIGNED EDITION IS ALSO AVAILABLE.**

Deborah Biancotti

4

THIS IS COPY

Waking in Winter

Waking in Winter

DEBORAH BIANCOTTI

WAKING IN WINTER Copyright © 2016 Deborah Biancotti
COVER ART Copyright © 2016 Amanda Rainey

Published in March 2016 by PS Publishing Ltd. by arrangement with
the author. All rights reserved by the author. The right of Deborah
Biancotti to be identified as Author of this Work has been asserted
by her in accordance with the Copyright, Designs and Patents Act 1988.

First Edition

ISBN
978-1-84863-917-1 (Signed Edition)
978-1-84863-916-4

This book is a work of fiction. Names, characters, places and incidents either are
products of the author's imagination or are used fictitiously. Any resemblance to
actual events or locales or persons, living or dead, is entirely coincidental.

Design and layout by Alligator Tree Graphics.
Printed in England by T. J. International.

PS Publishing Ltd / Grosvenor House / 1 New Road / Hornsea, HU18 1PG / England

editor@pspublishing.co.uk / www.pspublishing.co.uk

For those that taught me how to survive the cold

If winter hadn't been about to burst, if it hadn't been her last flight, if she hadn't been scheduled to go home in two days. If the icy desert beneath her hadn't looked so deeply flawless that morning (hard white rock whipped by a layer of fresh snow like Pashmak). If she hadn't turned north instead of south she might never have seen it.

If she'd kept quiet they might never have found out.

"Muir, say again?" A voice from Base cut across the other conversations in her helmet, sinking them to a soft burr.

She hadn't meant to give herself away. But her breath had caught at the sight, and her sigh had triggered the radio. Otherwise, she might've gotten away with it.

The radio buzzed constantly across Muir's skull like a low-grade migraine. She could hear the glacionauts hundreds of metres beneath the ice surface talking to the researchers in the labs back at Base. She heard the occasional driver and pilot checking coordinates. She'd gotten so used to the noise she couldn't sleep without it.

"Muir?"

She'd been filling in time, following random scars in the skin of permafrost beneath her, watching the ice floes the way she used to watch clouds as a kid. Looking for a shape. She was less claustrophobic in her twin-seater Otter than back at Base.

"Nothing, Base," she replied. "I didn't say anything."

Base Station wasn't deterred. "Muir? Why are you so far north?"

Base Station's voice sounded clipped and hollow in the helmet, wasp-buzzing and flat. But she could still spot the annoyance in—his? she thought it was his—tone. He was tired, probably. Bored, like they all were. Otherwise he wouldn't have checked her coordinates. You're not off course if nobody knows you're off course.

"The hell, Muir?" A different voice in the helmet. Partholon, riding meltwater somewhere beneath an ice shelf. "Tell me you found some kind of mythical wreck so we can ride it out of this mess of a place."

Static that was probably laughter. It was his favourite joke, the one about escaping. But like all of them, Partholon had nowhere else to go.

"Muir," Base again, "you've travelled well outside your grid. Return immediately. And," one last imperative added in a soft growl, "stop wasting our goddamn fuel."

Base Station clicked to silence. There was no need to say more, nobody expected Muir to ignore a command. But she spun in a slow circle, angling the wings of her Otter at 45 degrees to the ground so she could look out through the hexagon of windows that pressed in on her.

In the ice, long tendrils of blue-white *something* showed like veins, like seaweed. No, like hair. Miles of hair that lazily curled around a giant face carved into the ice. A woman's face, pointed chin and wide lips and sloping eyes. The figure's left lobe caught a flash of light as Muir passed. It shone like a pearl.

"Wait," Muir said, buying time. She cleared her throat. "It looks like a..."

Goddess.

She was cold, but she was used to cold. She'd been made numb by it months ago. Staring at the figure beneath her was like the most painful thawing she could imagine.

"Holy, Mary, Mother," Muir whispered. She couldn't help it.

"There's one for the daily broadsheet," Partholon shouted. "Muir's found religion."

She coasted alongside a giant shoulder in the ice, nosing the outline of a bare arm and the swoop of a sterile breast, the curve of an elbow where it cupped a smooth, white belly.

Muir pulled the rover up higher until it skimmed six then eight metres above the ground. She discovered where the pale white scales began beneath the icy figure's wrist, just above a swell like a hip. She followed the three metres it took to reach the frozen fan of a tail, six metres across at its edge and delicately curled. Almost beckoning.

"Jesus, it's a mermaid," she whispered.

A hoot of laughter from Partholon. "I knew it, I knew Muir was losing her mind!"

"Vipond, go check on Muir." Base must have grown tired of waiting.

"Already on my way, Base."

Muir skimmed the other side of the mermaid and found a jagged edge at the end of her arm. Her hand had been taken off at the wrist.

A fierce possessiveness flooded through her. It clogged her throat and put a tremble in her hands. She circled back to the brow.

The almond curve of icy eyes watched her as she approached, early morning light dancing along blue-white irises. Muir wanted to curl up in the blank pupils. She could sleep for a thousand years in those eyes. She could slip along those pastel lashes and lie on those crystalline cheeks.

They couldn't take the mermaid from her.

She tried to sound casual. "I made a mistake. Must be the glare. Vipond, return to Base—"

"Too late, I'm already here."

Vipond's Otter swung into view over her tail, black wings on a red-bellied twin-seater. He headed right for her, too fast and too close. He must have been looking at the ground; he must have found the mermaid.

"Look out!" Muir banked sharply to avoid colliding with the distracted Vipond.

His countermove brought him close to the ground. The beetle-black wing of his plane sent up a wing of shaved ice.

"Sweet Jesus, Muir," Vipond muttered. He was Buddhist, but they'd all been together too long. "Sweet freaking Jesus!"

"Do you see it?" Muir asked, her voice timid. A swell of something like pride rose through her.

She was thrilled to be sharing it, the mermaid. Even not wanting to, even wanting to hoard it for herself.

"I see something," Vipond confirmed. "I sure as hell don't know what it is. Base, I'm landing."

"Oh, great," Base said. "Don't *land* if you don't know what it is. Those are expensive planes you're flying."

"Muir, Mother of God, tell us. Are we going home or aren't we?" Partholon was milking it for all he had.

"Negative, Partholon. There is no pirate ship here."

The buzz of laughter followed Muir down.

She flipped on her distress signal so Base would get a clear reading on her landing position. The engine let out a high-pitched squeal as she lowered it to the ice beside the face of the mermaid, to where a perfect clear freckle touched the corner of her right temple.

Vipond was already out of his plane, stalking to the edge of the mermaid's hair despite the below-freezing temperatures. He jogged towards the mermaid's face. Muir joined him, dry ice slipping and squeaking under her feet.

She flipped open her helmet and looked up at him. Out here, far from Base, the air was sharply clean, empty of any scent except for what they brought. Vipond smelled of soap.

She pulled the thermal layer of her inner mask up to her eyes. Despite that, she felt the bitter, dry cold pour into her helmet. It gripped her face and throat and made her eyes burn. Sunlight danced before her, almost solid. Out here the glare could blind for days, floating like bright ghouls in the vision.

"What do you see, Vipond?" she asked.

Vipond was muzzled in dark thermal layering like she was, a thin strip of deep-brown skin visible around his eyes. She could make out a frown as he shaded his eyes and leaned down. "What?"

"In the ice," Muir shouted through her muffling thermals, "do you see a woman?"

He made his way towards where the severed hand would be. Muir jogged to keep up.

"A woman? No." He shook his head. "I see a..."

"Yeah?"

"A lotus flower."

"A what?"

"Four, six storeys high if it was a building. Wide enough to park a couple buses. It's amazing."

"A lotus flower?" she asked.

He held his gloved hand up in front of him, index finger tapping his thumb in a nervous staccato. He didn't answer.

She grabbed his arm. "Wait, you see a lotus flower?"

"Yeah. Don't you? It's a Buddhist thing, Muir. All the way out here, a sign from Siddhartha."

Muir shivered. She pulled her helmet closed and wrapped her arms around herself, but the shivering wouldn't go away.

The cold had gotten into her bones. She breathed in the sickly, tangy smell that came from working on a base station, everything trapped in her clothes and helmet.

Beside them the mermaid's open eyes stared impassively up at the grey tin sky.

A lotus flower?

Vipond was using his free hand to trace out the shape of the flower in the air, its broad petals upright. His dark eyes shone from between the gap in his thermal mask. Behind him the white morning sky was giving way to a swirl of deeper grey. A storm was coming.

"There's no lotus flower here, Vipond."

He was ignoring her.

Muir felt something slip inside her. The beginning of an avalanche.

"T̲ʜᴇ ʀᴀᴛs ᴀʀᴇ ᴄᴏᴍɪɴɢ," Vɪᴘᴏɴᴅ ᴍᴜᴛᴛᴇʀᴇᴅ.

He was talking about the lab rats, the scientists. Dragged up from under glaciers or the warm insides of Base Station Un to witness the discovery.

They'd retired to her plane. Inside was no warmer than out, but at least it stopped the wind. A thin skein of ice coated the windshield in lacework patterns. Clouds had come to settle not far from them. Up close the clouds were more grit than fluff, a kind of grey haze made dirty by the startling white of the snow.

Muir turned the volume down on her radio until it became a low, comforting hum. She closed her eyes and in the bright winter whiteness, the insides of her lids glowed red. She pressed her thumbs to her lids, blackening them.

"Got a headache?" Vipond asked, beside her.

"Constantly."

He chuckled. Muir liked Vipond. Usually he didn't have to talk so much, but the mermaid must have unsettled him. The lotus flower. Otherwise, he could sit quietly through an entire evening, an entire day, saying nothing that wasn't necessary. She wished today was one of those days.

"Gonna make it home in time for the funeral?" he asked.

Muir started. She tried not to answer but his stare held her.

"They're holding off," she said. "Waiting for me to get home."

"That's nice."

"Yeah." She supposed it was.

Vipond checked his watch. "This is going to take hours."

"You can head back to Base if you like. I'll wait here."

He didn't even consider it. "Nah."

She knew how he felt. It was impossible to leave. This far out, the desert of ice had a life of its own. It dwarfed them, laying out so many textures and shades that every other place she'd been since had felt riotous, dense with colour and noise. Here, the fissures and shelves of ice allowed her mind to flow, to follow. Each slip and sloe was like a welt in the thick skin of ice.

"Were you close with your mother?" Vipond asked.

Still going on about the funeral. Muir shifted in her seat.

"No."

"Will it be a traditional Japanese funeral or—"

"Hey, feet," Partholon's voice again, "this is a nice catch-up we're having. I feel so close to you guys."

"Go to hell, Partholon." Muir switched off her radio.

He cackled. "Too late. Already there."

Vipond mouthed 'sorry' to her, then switched off his own radio and sat, hands curled into each other on his thigh.

'Feet' was Partholon's word for the pilots, a play on their job descriptions as 'basic foot patrol'. Probably also because they were dispensable. Other people called them rover-pilots, rovers, dogs. Depending.

"You don't want to go home?" Vipond asked.

Muir sighed, short and sharp. "That whole planet can burn for all I care."

"That's harsh."

"Can we not talk about this?"

"I just thought, for your mother's sake—"

"Vipond, if you don't shut up I'm throwing you out of here."

He was quiet. "Okay."

A red Spryte came bumping and hurtling across the uneven drifts, scattering snow. It was one of the smaller kind, built for a group of about six, and could have passed for regular SUVs with a tray on its back, except for the belted, triangular wheels.

"I'll be damned." A new voice over the radio. Waterman. She was probably driving the Spryte. "I'll be double-dog damned, look what we found. A pair of feet, kicking back and enjoying the day."

She hooted with laughter at her own joke.

"We came to see your mermaid, Muir," she continued.

Waterman recited fish recipes as she exited the Spryte. Two others climbed out with her. They wore bright orange and red and purple, colours that clashed with the landscape.

Partholon was one of them, Muir realised with a sinking stomach.

"You feet must be out of your minds," Partholon said. "This is miles from anywhere, what were you even doing here?"

"I was chasing Muir," Vipond said into his reactivated radio.

Hoots and jeers went up along the radio channel. Muir cursed and gave him the bird. Vipond winked like they were sharing a joke. He clambered out of the passenger seat. There was a blast of cold air as he opened the Otter door. He stepped out onto the wing, nimble as a dancer.

The last person out of Waterman's Spryte was a surprise. She wore the unmistakable red-on-white cross of the medic on her narrow back. Rare to see her so far from Base. Adriatico, nicknamed Medici. She hated open spaces, said she preferred the comforting constriction of a good wound any day to the blunt contusion of the outside world. She stood by the Spryte, resting an elbow against its metal wall while the others took off towards the mermaid's sleeping shape.

"Quite the looker," Partholon shouted through her closed Otter window.

Muir knew it was the lead-up to another joke. "Yeah?"

Partholon obliged. "I meant Medici. Not your invisible mermaid."

"Shut-up, Partholon," Adriatico said through the comms.

Vipond straightened, still standing on the wing. Like he was trying to get a better view.

"Lotus flower," Muir spat. "As if."

The mermaid was huge, only visible from the air. From where Partholon stood he might, if he was observant, find the point where her neck curved between jaw and shoulder, her hair cushioning her from the ice.

Muir had thought it might be trapped under the ice. An enormous sculpture, perhaps. Captured in white stone.

Which made the missing hand even more strange and impossible. Regardless of how heavy or light the stone was, the sheer scale of her missing hand would have made mechanical intervention probable. Even required. Across this stark, slippery landscape a dozen humans couldn't have moved something that size very far.

Unless they'd destroyed it. Maybe the hand was shattered among the rocks already, snow disguising the fingers as if they were part of the already destroyed landscape. Perhaps someone had ruined it out of jealousy. Or out of fear.

The ice was like a curtain, it cut off what happened here from what happened everywhere else. It made it easier to believe that this was a dream, a fantasy, and the rest of their lives were something else.

"What is it, something in the ice?" Waterman asked.

Sitting there slant-on to the mermaid's face, Muir felt she knew better. This close, she could tell. The mermaid, it wasn't *in* the ice. It was *of* the ice.

She hunkered further into her Otter. She thought perhaps the rest of the planet had formed around this mermaid and her broken hand.

Partholon moved back and forth on the ice, kicking up permafrost and sneering all around him.

"Hey, Partholon, what do you see from there?" she asked into the radio.

Partholon grunted. "Looks like a face."

"You see a woman?" Muir asked, too quickly.

"What? No, hell, no. This face isn't human. I see…I'm telling you…"

But Partholon didn't tell her. He continued to pace, drawing out the shapes he found on a notebook, alternately cursing and muttering.

"What about you, Waterman?" Muir persisted

"A giant fish," Waterman said with emphasis. "But that could be because I'm starving. Lucky I'm not seeing pizza, I'd have a mouthful of dry ice by now."

Waterman stubbed a toe in the ground. Across the rest of the white landscape, nothing moved.

Muir tried not to sound desperate. "Adriatico? See anything?"

A pause while Adriatico adjusted the radio inside her sturdy red coat. "I can see something human."

Muir estimated that Adriatico was crouching beside the mermaid's ear.

"Care to elaborate, Medici?" Vipond used the medic's nickname.

"Someone bearded, I think."

Muir sat up straighter in her plane. "Hey, Adriatico. You Christian?"

She saw through the glass windows Adriatico turn to look at her plane. Her hands dangled between her knees. Her head was inclined to the side like she was contemplating not the question, but the questioner. Despite her dark goggles, Muir could feel her stare.

"Catholic, yeah," said Adriatico. "Why?"

Partholon cut through. "Holy crap, this thing has horns. Holy crap, Muir. You've found Satan himself."

There was a pause while everyone held their breath, stilled as if the ice had reached into their lungs. And then Partholon burst out laughing.

A couple of Humvees arrived, fat wheels slapping up snow. More scientists come to see what Muir had found.

There was jealous joking as they approached, all envy and wounded pride. A foot wasn't supposed to discover things. A foot was supposed to ferry the scientists. Let the rats do the discovering.

The scientists wore thick-spiked climbing boots that couldn't possibly pierce the ice enough to touch the mermaid. Still, Muir winced.

She watched the rats in their yellow fatigues lean against Waterman's red Spryte, just far enough from Adriatico they didn't have to include her in conversation. Nobody trusted Base doctors.

Bayoumi, senior rat, approached Muir's rover. She watched him come on. Over his head, she could see Vipond head towards the other rats. Trying to form alliances. He was itching to go back up, she could tell. He needed the order, though, like she did. He must have spotted Bayoumi at her Otter, because he became still. Impossible to read his expression or even see his face under the thermal masks. But she could guess at it.

In the end, it was as much that as anything else that made her agree to what came next.

When Bayoumi was close enough, she slid the hatch. A shunt of frosted air rolled over her.

"Can you take me up?" Bayoumi asked. "Quick tour? Faster than in that old Spryte, eh?"

He affected a note of camaraderie. He was bronzed and dark-eyed. His smile seemed almost warm under his icy beard. Muir wanted to say no. An old instinct, defence against the rats. They always wanted to go where they didn't belong and take what didn't belong to them.

But at least with Bayoumi in the Otter, she'd get another look at her mermaid.

"Fine," she said. "Get in."

She waved at Vipond. He didn't wave back.

Bayoumi was sure on his feet for a big man. He levered himself into the passenger seat. His third trip to the ice, he still had excess fat on his middle. She sent the Otter out and up.

They toured the ice-locked figure more than once. Muir was ready to keep flying until they ran out of fuel or Bayoumi ordered her out of the sky. One or the other. The mermaid watched her with intent, pale eyes.

Bayoumi broke the silence. "Eighteen metres tall, wouldn't you say?"

He didn't wait for Muir's agreement.

"Fascinating," he said. "We'll have our work cut out for us digging her up."

"You see her?"

"Of course. And I know who she is," Bayoumi beamed.

The Otter was so small his knees almost reached his chest.

"Who?" Muir asked.

"The goddess Sekhmet."

"Who?" Muir asked again.

Bayoumi didn't seem to hear. "And on a planet so distant from our own. Remarkable, isn't it? Makes you think... well. All sorts of things. About the reach of gods. And people. It makes you wonder, too, about what we believe."

Muir waited. "Okay, Bayoumi. Wonder, how?"

"Well." Bayoumi shifted, trying to lean towards her. "We thought we were the first humans. But if so, how did Sekhmet get here? Either we aren't, and other humans before us brought the goddess. Or..."

Bayoumi seemed lost in the sight beneath them.

"Or?" Muir prompted.

"Ah," Bayoumi replied. "Or, our beliefs didn't originate on Earth. They were carried to us by... some other race before us. You see?"

Muir frowned. "No, I don't."

"You understand," Bayoumi held out pleading hands, "we must wonder if our beliefs originated here or there."

"Okay."

"Where is the origin of this most ancient belief? You see?"

"Check." Muir's hands on the steering unit were still. "I'm not familiar with this... Sekhmet?"

"She is an Egyptian goddess, a powerful one. Goddess of war, for instance. Not such a positive province, but," Bayoumi shrugged, "we would be wise not to upset her."

Muir almost laughed. "How do you know for sure it's her?"

"From the headdress. She has the face of a lion in profile. See?"

Muir gazed down into the serene white eyes of the mermaid. Her icy chin was tilted like she was bowing. Or listening.

"I don't see a lion," Muir said.

"No? Interesting. Perhaps you need to know the mythology to see it. I can show you pictures at Base."

They flew through the grey air in silence.

"So, you're a big believer, Bayoumi?"

"In Egyptian mythology? Not so much, I suppose. Of course, we are taught at school in Egypt. My parents believed, I think. My mother." He smiled. "We scientists, however, we cannot afford to believe. We must *know*."

Muir moved awkwardly. She found something paternal in Bayoumi. The calm readiness of his smile and his unselfconscious way of moving. His broad girth and his hands like plates.

She meant to tell him she could see something different in the ice. She wanted to. She meant to say she'd noticed they all saw something different, each one of them who'd made the pilgrimage to the mermaid.

"Bayoumi?"

"Yes?"

A scientist, she reminded herself, must know. And so the moment slipped away. She felt it go, sloughing off her skin.

"Nothing."

Bayoumi had already turned his attention back to the windows and the shape freeze-dried below them.

"We will dig her up," he said. "It will be quite a thing."

"Can't you study her here, in the ice shelf?"

Bayoumi didn't even respond. Muir understood what drove him then, and she believed—she knew—it wasn't science. It was the mermaid or the goddess or whatever he thought he was looking at. There was something about the trapped figure that itched. The indifferent beauty, the unnatural stillness, the perfection that made her hard to hold onto. She wanted to be free.

As if at any moment the mermaid's chest might rise to draw breath. She might blink those opal eyes that surely held sugar-white images of the ocean behind their lids.

"Who's gonna fund that, then?" Van der Zee spat.

Van der Zee was practical. No one got to be captain of a base station without being practical. His voice was commanding, even on the radio. All other static stilled. All voices were quietened by his.

Muir looked over at Bayoumi, slouched sideways in the driver's seat of the Humvee. His elbow was high on the steering wheel. His orange parka filled the space.

Behind them the others sat, equally gigantic, jackets brushing though their arms were crossed or straight by their sides. Bayoumi moved the two-way to his face and clicked it on.

"Who will know?" he said. "We record an exploratory nautical dig, tell them it turned up nothing."

Van der Zee couldn't see Bayoumi's broad gestures, the way he rolled his head like he was haggling on the price of something.

Van der Zee said, "Sooner or later they're going to start asking. I mean really asking, Bayoumi. Remember, there's meant to be no drilling. Some kind of goddamned treaty."

"No mineral drilling." Bayoumi held up a finger like he was lecturing a child. "*Mineral*. We're not taking any minerals away."

"How can you be sure?"

"If it is mineral, we'll put it back," Bayoumi beamed.

The others sniggered into their gloves.

Wind whipped ice along the windshield. Outside, Muir's Otter was awash with a foam of snow. Behind Bayoumi, Waterman fiddled with her pack and ignored Partholon's clumsy advances. In the very back, Vipond and Adriatico were crammed in together while the wind hurled outside the Humvee.

"So this thing," Van der Zee began. "This—"

"Artefact," Bayoumi supplied.

"There's no way it consists of anything mineral?"

Bayoumi's eyebrows knitted together. He glanced around the inside of the Humvee once, for support.

"We could send one drill directly into her for assurance," Bayoumi said, his tone doubtful.

"No!"

Muir's voice was louder than she meant it to be. She pretended not to notice Bayoumi's sharp gesture in her direction. She knew what the quick flick of his wrist meant, and the tight shake of his head. It meant she should know her place.

Muir added, "We might damage her."

Partholon's head snapped up. "Ooooh, look at the feet, stomping all over the rats—"

He was stopped by a swipe of Vipond's arm.

"I can come up with something," Bayoumi said in the radio. "Leave it with me."

Silence from Van der Zee.

It was an uneasy truce they lived in. In real ways, they relied on each other for survival. It spoiled you, this kind of work. It made it impossible to work anyplace that wasn't temporary. Even a base camp could feel too permanent, compared to an Otter.

Muir had worked these jobs for nearly a decade. She knew better than to jeopardise her good reputation. But desperation did funny things. Made the future seem like it might be far away.

The radio crackled to life.

"It'll be dark in two days," Van der Zee said. "I can't imagine you being able to operate drills that far out. Let alone lights as well."

Bayoumi was still. "I'll take responsibility."

"I know it," Van der Zee replied. "Stick a flag in the damn thing and return to Base. Right now."

The radio clicked once, loudly, and Van der Zee was gone.

"He never says good-bye, anyone else notice that?" Partholon was philosophical.

"He's right," Vipond said from the back. "It'll be winter in two days. We'll be drilling in the dark."

Bayoumi was thoughtful, clicking the radio on and off with his thumb, weighing his options.

"A storm's coming. Isn't it, Muir?"

Muir nodded yes without thinking.

Vipond's voice joined hers reluctantly. "We can't leave the Otters out here any longer. Van der Zee will have our skins."

And then he'd make sure they never made it onto another research base, anywhere, ever again.

Bayoumi said, "Is that true?"

He was looking at Muir. She felt more than saw Vipond's restless unhappiness from the back.

"Yeah," she said. "It is."

"We all better head back." Bayoumi nodded. "Wait out the storm."

Muir was out of the Humvee before Bayoumi finished speaking. Another chance to walk past the mermaid.

The sky darkened and the winds stabbed and curled. Vipond cursed with each step, but he came along, too. The storm whipped frost into their eyes.

Vipond struggled with his goggles, bending low so his hood covered his face. Behind them the Humvee revved its engine and began a slow circuit back towards Base.

Muir said, "Everybody sees something different."

Vipond stopped cursing. "What?"

"In the ice," Muir continued. "Something to do with what we believe in, I think. Or what we were taught, or something. Maybe," she hesitated, "one of our first beliefs."

Vipond adjusted his goggles and pulled up the thermal mask to meet them.

"You were serious about the mermaid?" he asked.

"Yeah, I was serious. What did you think I was?"

She waited. He was probably about to ask her what that meant, the mermaid. But she didn't know herself.

Instead, he grunted. "I wonder what in hell Partholon saw."

"Ducks," Partholon said.

"You saw ducks?" Muir asked. "What does that mean?"

They were in the mess hall, grimy with the smells of boiling potato and frying sausages, and the diesel that clung to their clothes, every one of them.

Outside they all wore thick parkas and trousers, even Adriatico if she ever went outside. But inside they stripped down to black skivvies and thermals. Most kept their white boots on. The floor was almost always wet, and in cold this pervasive, water could kill the way ice and wind killed.

Partholon held a tube of something gelatinous that he claimed was dessert-flavoured. His cousin had sent it. Space food, the cousin called it. Partholon thought it was hilarious. More hilarious than delicious, apparently, because the tube remained largely unconsumed.

The usual cliques and divisions showed themselves on every other table but theirs. Rats with rats. Feet and other admin staff gathered around tables dragged together in clumsy design. Admin outnumbered scientists three to one, always did. Everyone thought they ran the place, didn't matter what job they held down.

A fish tank sat in one corner, full of water but empty of fish. An inflatable palm tree, deflating, stood limply propped against one wall. It was surrounded by sagging beach balls. The beach balls had become a tradition. New ones kept appearing. People kept denying responsibility. Opposite the palm was a dartboard that regularly featured one or other of the higher-ups from HQ. The darts had long since been pilfered, and the board was so pockmarked it was hard to tell the colours.

"I *wish* I saw ducks." Partholon grinned. "Might explain where all my damn ducks are going."

Outside, the sky was dust-grey, though the clocks around the room showed nine at night. The buildings that made up Base Camp had the subdued hum of expectation. In every residential corridor there was the rustle of packing as people readied to leave before winter clamped down.

"You *still* losing all those yellow rubber ducks?" Vipond sneered. "There's a joke in that. Something about yellow snow."

Partholon ignored him. In Partholon's world, only he made the jokes. "Or one giant mother of a duck. Like, a godmother of ducks."

Vipond persisted. "Why can't you find any of those stupid ducks again? Don't you have theories on the water flow under the surface?"

"Of course we have theories," Partholon snapped. "The ducks are meant to *prove* the theories. We estimate the water to be flowing in a certain direction and therefore exiting at a particular place. We drop a few ducks into a sinkhole, we go to the place where the ducks should come out."

Partholon hated to explain his research. Vipond liked to make Partholon do things he hated.

"And?" Vipond asked. "Where are the ducks?"

"Damned if I know," Partholon said through gritted teeth.

There was a snigger around the table.

"This godforsaken place," Partholon continued, "maybe the damn ice eats them."

"Yeah," Vipond agreed. "Somewhere out there is some duck-flavoured ice with your name on it, Partholon."

"I never eat yellow ice, my friend," Partholon held up a hand, Scout's honour–style. "I got your yellow-snow joke right here!"

Around the table, the snigger turned to a warm-hearted laugh. Even Adriatico joined in. Something about the day had made a team out of them. Van der Zee would be pleased to see it. Always going on about teamwork.

Adriatico met Muir's eye. "You have a theory on all this?"

Muir shook her head. She had no theory. She had nothing.

Bayoumi joined them, his tray piled high with red, soaked carbohydrates that had probably been intended as spaghetti bolognese. He chewed thoughtlessly, eyes glazed. Muir knew how he felt.

"You?" Muir asked Adriatico.

"None."

Van der Zee came towards them. He was a commanding figure, the white zinc on his face matching the white-grey of his hair and eyes. He stood loosely in his orange snow gear, managing to look like a king in clothes that made others look like obese jockeys.

"Been outside, sir?" Muir asked.

The others sniggered. 'Sir' wasn't something people used a lot. Muir liked it. It helped provide a structure to a world that was all white chaos.

"Prepping a Seal," Van der Zee nodded. "Turns out, I have to head home for a few days. My sister has died."

There was silence. No one had heard this level of intimacy from him before. No one knew what to do with it.

Bayoumi rose to his feet and reached out a hand. Van der Zee shook it and kept shaking, his face like iron.

"I'm sorry to hear of your loss," Bayoumi said.

Van der Zee thanked him and kept pumping Bayoumi's hand like maybe he hoped this would tie him more firmly to the ground. Like maybe he was about to be lost to the atmosphere, or the grief.

He caught Muir staring.

"What about you? Want to catch the next flight out with me?" he asked. "Leaving in twenty minutes."

Muir was embarrassed. He'd remembered.

"Later," she said.

"Have you missed the funeral?"

"No, they're holding it for me."

Van der Zee didn't flinch, which made her feel worse.

"How long you expect the family to hold off?" he asked.

"I'm the only family."

Van der Zee shook his head in something like disappointment. She met his stare. It was none of his business.

Bayoumi interrupted. "I've had an idea. About the artefact."

Van der Zee's gaze snapped around. "That's not what we're here for."

"But it should be," Bayoumi replied. He bobbed his head. "We're missing an opportunity to learn about this place. What culture happened here, what moved the people who lived here."

"If they even *were* people," Partholon muttered.

"And finally," Bayoumi ignored him, "what made them leave."

Van der Zee shifted his weight. "You're about to start arguing morals again, doctor. It's outside your scope. We're here on behalf of a multibillion-dollar corporation. You think they care about morals?"

"How about this." Partholon eased upwards from his seat. "We tell them we've found a great tourist attraction. Tell them to imagine the crowds that'll want to see the place where we discovered a damn religious artefact, for chrissake. They pay to dig her up, pay to ship her wherever, pay for research. If that's what you want, Bayoumi?"

"Won't they just want to leave her where she is?" Waterman said. "There's your tourist attraction right there."

"I'm with Waterman," Muir said.

"No, but Partholon is right," Bayoumi said. "We could extract her for research purposes. Then donate her to a museum. It happens all the time. We tell them this is now a holy site, but here is your relic, carefully preserved. Two tourist sites for the price of one."

"And twice the income." Partholon leaned forward to slap Muir backhanded across the shoulder. "See? I'm right, aren't I?"

All eyes were on Van der Zee, even Bayoumi's, though he tried to pretend indifference. That was how Bayoumi always won his arguments, by making his opponent believe the outcome didn't matter.

Van der Zee gave no sign he'd even heard Partholon, which in itself was probably the greatest giveaway. At last he issued a curt nod.

"I'm leaving this in your hands, Bayoumi, as second-in-command while I'm gone." He raised his hand to point. "You have one week until I'm back."

"One week," Bayoumi beamed. "And two days until dark."

"How will you get back?" Muir asked. "Won't they stop all flights over winter?"

"Not once I explain to them that every one of you is insane and can't be trusted," Van der Zee grumbled. "But I'll do that after the funeral."

They were quiet, not even sniggering.

Van der Zee turned back to Muir.

"Last chance, Muir. Should go for your mother. Let her rest in peace."

Muir nodded. "Sir."

His stare bore into her for another moment. Then he turned to face whatever was waiting for him at home.

Watching him leave felt like an ending Muir hadn't prepared for. The end of reason, she thought. Without him, Bayoumi was almost certainly going to start drilling. Better to ask forgiveness than permission, Bayoumi always said. It made him a successful scientist and a real son of a bitch to disagree with.

Partholon gave her a dirty sneer. "Penny for your thoughts, Muir."

He pushed something across the table towards her. A perfect origami mermaid.

Muir began to clear her tray.

"What's the matter? Don't want to go home? Don't want to confront the dead?"

"Shut up, Partholon," Vipond muttered. "Feet outnumber rats, two to one."

Muir dropped her tray into the cleaning bins. When she left the mess hall—back straight, shoulders tight like a woman with a purpose—she heard Partholon laugh and call out something that was hushed by the other voices at the table.

He'd called her *baby killer*.

She was up early or she hadn't slept, one of the two. Whatever fugue state she'd spent the night in had been filled with shadows and strange shapes. She'd been wrapped in strands of sea spray, rocked by ice like air, like water.

Her mother had been with her for part of it, and the moments after she'd left had been filled with a wracking grief that Muir had never felt in her waking life.

She skipped the mess hall breakfast and made her way to the hangars, following the smell of oil and diesel. Her Otter had survived the storm with only a few new scrapes. She'd expected an angry confrontation from the engineers or de Marinis, the hangar manager, for waiting so long to return it, but no one said anything.

Moving into the hangar, she had the feeling she'd become invisible. The place was buzzing with conversation about what had been found in the ice. No one acknowledged her. No one mentioned it was her discovery. Even the find itself had taken on the mystique of the divine.

She smoothed her hand along the underbelly of the Otter and across its blunt-sloped nose. Something like gratitude pushed against her breast.

"Taking her up again?"

So she wasn't invisible after all.

Bayoumi was red-eyed with lack of sleep, his cheeks unshaven, the narrow beard that lined his jaw twisted into untidy plaits.

"You need a ride someplace?" Muir smiled.

Bayoumi smiled back automatically, like it was purely social, his mind travelling to some other place. But then reason returned sharply to his dark eyes and he frowned, looking at her more closely.

"What's your interest?" he asked.

Muir, if anyone, understood his suspicion. She got it. She shared his need to both revisit the remarkable thing in the ice and keep it to himself. The possessiveness had him. But she needed him to approve her use of the Otter in Van der Zee's absence, so she shrugged and smiled.

"What's your interest, Bayoumi?" she asked.

Checkmate. Bayoumi's smile widened, but it didn't look like a smile anymore. He nodded to the Otter.

"How long do you need to prep?" he asked.

"How fast can you get in?"

It was part bluster. Muir still needed to refuel. But short minutes later they were rolling past the hangar door and out into a morning that looked suspiciously like the day before. Like every day before that. The sun might have been lower in the south, but not enough to gauge by human eye. Shadows stretched long towards them across frosty ground that looked impossible, insubstantial. The cold crowded them.

"Hard to believe it'll be dark in two days," Bayoumi muttered.

"If you count today," Muir replied.

She steered the Otter along familiar, invisible lines, gunning the engine in a steadily improving speed, adjusting the wing flaps up to catch the air and twist it under and around her plane.

They shot upwards into the glare of sunlight. At this moment and rarely any other moment, Muir felt free. Like she might dissolve up here.

"I did some research," Bayoumi said.

"On whoever lived here before us?"

"No," Bayoumi hesitated. "There's no record of that."

Muir waited. "On her?"

"Sekhmet," he confirmed. "Goddess of war. Also, it transpires, goddess of pestilence and destruction."

"Well, I guess that follows."

"And the desert," Bayoumi concluded.

"Any desert in particular? Or just all of them?"

"Do you know the definition of a desert?" Bayoumi asked. He didn't give her time to answer. "Less than five hundred millimetres of rain in a standard year. Do you know how much this place gets?"

"I'm guessing, less than that?"

"Your guess is correct."

"So, what are we doing here, then? I mean, what can a desert ice planet possibly provide for us?"

"Oh, you never know what you'll find. Bacteria, for one thing. Perhaps some of which will carry cures or will help us build better human immune systems. Do you understand?"

Muir nodded. She understood, she always had. They were here to find reasons to exploit it, this bright, sharp, beautiful place.

Beneath them the wide, flat tundra began to give way to ground that was more ragged and rocky, pockmarked with cliffs that poked grey through the hoarfrost.

It was here the cold really set in. Here their bulky suits at last began to feel more like necessity than inconvenience.

Beneath them the earth dipped sharply to reveal a grey bluff. Beneath it was *Mer de Glace*, named after a similar ocean from home. The ocean was buried under an ice shelf so thick no one had ever reached it. They guessed it was there from the shape, not from the evidence of water.

Surrounding the frozen ocean were hard-faced crags and mountains no one had gotten around to naming yet. They were streaked with brown dirt, squeezed up from someplace under all that ice. Blue, brown, grey. The only other colours this place afforded, invigorated by the fact of their rarity.

"How come there are oceans here?" Muir asked. "And lakes? I mean, if it's a desert."

"They were laid down before the rain dried up, I guess," Bayoumi said. "Or they've been building for centuries, drawing tiny amounts of whatever precious water they could find. You'll have to ask Partholon."

Muir reflected she probably wouldn't.

Bayoumi was leaning towards the window beside him, round shoulders even more rounded, forehead to the glass with the houndstooth fur of his parka between them. He looked abandoned, an overgrown child crammed into the tiny space of the Otter.

"You think you'll try drilling it out?" Muir asked.

"Of course."

"How long will that take?"

"To release the whole form? The rest of my life." He laughed and sat up and rubbed a gloved hand across his face.

"Maybe you don't need to dig her up," Muir said.

It felt redundant.

She delayed the inevitable by flying north, further and further north until they'd tipped back around the very top of the world and were heading south again. Couldn't help but head south.

Bayoumi didn't comment. He wasn't used to the landscape this high up. He wouldn't be able to tell one direction from another, one landscape from its cousins.

She held off returning to the spot where the mermaid lay. Not just to delay his satisfaction but because she was afraid. What if the mermaid was gone?

The longer she delayed, the greater the nagging in her gut became. What if she'd been taken while they slept? What if she had been part of the dream?

"Why do they call you baby killer?" Bayoumi asked.

Muir jumped. So hard the Otter rocked. Bayoumi had to brace himself with both hands on the dash.

"Sorry," she said.

"No, me, I apologise," Bayoumi said. He eased back into his chair. "I meant, because I know it was an accident. Why are people so cruel in that Base station, eh? That is my question."

Muir figured it was probably a reflection of the cold cruelty of the world outside Base. She'd been here for months. The only living things she'd seen were the people she worked with. The only sign of any other life was the mermaid, buried deep in the ice.

"They call me that because they know I hate it," Muir said. "What other reason do they need?"

Bayoumi grunted. He gave her a thoughtful look. Muir kept her eyes on the landscape wedged between her windows.

She shouldn't have answered, she figured. She should have let him come up with his own theories. Bayoumi seemed like a benevolent guy. He probably wouldn't have wondered if she'd just left it alone.

He turned his attention to the windows again. They had cleared the ocean and were rushing past the rugged faces of glaciers. Like frozen humpback giants, crammed together. With the sun behind them, the glaciers looked like a cityscape, white buildings crowding the sky, with roots so deep and thick they were blue at the base. The colour of the water they fed on.

They looked solid but Muir knew the glaciers moved. Unrooted, changing over time. It was part of what the rats studied. It was the reason people like Partholon existed, to chart and navigate and try to fix the ice. To predict it.

Cresting the last glacial ridge, she was about to coast above the ice cap where the mermaid lay. In the distance a lone flag announcing 'Base Station Un' stood limp in the absence of breeze.

"What's that?" Bayoumi asked suddenly.

He pointed, which was useless. Muir couldn't see out his windows without tipping the plane sideways. But she slowed and coasted around in an arc, giving Bayoumi longer to look at whatever he'd identified.

"It's the missing piece," Bayoumi nearly shouted. "It's the ankh from her hand."

"The what?"

He turned to Muir with a glittering gaze, his face victorious. "We found the missing piece."

Muir continued the arc, but now she was looking for a place to land. The wind had swept most of the snow from this area so she could see the rocky outlines of an old channel, now absent of whatever water had run there. She scooted the Otter along it and came to rest less than a dozen metres from the spot Bayoumi had identified.

He was out of the plane and across the ice, zipping up his jacket as he ran. Muir cursed and followed him, sending a curt message to Base to let them know she was following their current commanding officer outside. She flipped off the radio before anyone could reply.

When she caught up with Bayoumi he was standing still in the beat of the wind, his orange parka concave with the pressure of the gale. She was right beside him, sleeve to sleeve, before she saw it. In the ice, the goddess's hand. Palm open and upward like she might be cupping something coming from the sky. Fingers serenely reaching out, in repose. Nails neat and white like her skin was white. The hand itself was two metres long, almost a metre across from nail to nail. At Base Station they could probably use it for a lounge.

"This," Bayoumi said. "Now, this, we can dig up. In days, not months. A week, at most, probably."

He was almost babbling. The hand had been severed cleanly and moved. And then dropped, probably. Apart from that surgical cut, it seemed undamaged. Bayoumi, face unshielded, eyes wide and bright, looked at her with an expression as open and vulnerable as a child's.

"Can't we?" he said.

Muir felt fear march through her. She should be going home before winter came, to bury her mother. She should be leaving this place and its wide-open craziness. She should, most of all, be subject to the decisions of her superiors. Not making them.

She said, "Yes. We can dig this up."

They spent a day scoping the dig, shipping equipment from Base. It consumed all of them.

"Better than Christmas, Hallelujah," Vipond muttered, but Muir knew he felt the power of her, too.

For her own part, Muir hardly left the dig site. She didn't want the mermaid to be alone with them. She camped out in her Otter when she could, or hitched a ride with a Snow Cat when Base started counting her fuel.

She couldn't put into words exactly what made her do it. She was frightened. Of the obsession and of the mermaid who caused it. She felt like her ribs had turned to hollow ice.

Adriatico treated her for flu, though they agreed that wasn't what affected her. What she had was something deeper, something she couldn't shake.

"I half expect," said Adriatico, "he'll open his eyes and ask what all the noise is."

Muir laughed self-consciously and brushed a strand of black hair back into her braid. She nodded agreement, eyebrows raised at the unexpected camaraderie. Adriatico wrapped her in thin silver therma-sheets and let her be. It was probably all she could do.

Two days later, the darkness had claimed them. The last plane out of Base had left, and most of the Base population with it. Winter was there for good. For the next six months they were cut off, thrown back on their own resources.

Muir found herself thinking, *We're safe.*

Van der Zee vid-linked from a suburban lounge room back on Earth, the ice tan still visible around his eyes. He gave Muir a shocked, sad look. Worse than his expression was the fact he didn't say anything.

But by then they had all been consumed. Riding the adrenalin wave that emanated from the thing in the ice.

The drilling filled the waking hours of everyone in left Base Station Un for nearly three dark weeks. There was nothing else. The mealtimes that used to regulate Base began to disappear. The mess hall began to smell less and less of its customary boiling and frying. And the stink of diesel was everywhere, inside and out.

They worked for two weeks. They built a trench wide enough for equipment and personnel to take shelter. Then they carefully carved down and then around with heated saws, giving wide berth to the white skin of her hand. Bayoumi still called it an ankh. *The symbol of eternal life*, he told her.

They erected a temporary canvas above the drill site so the equipment could be protected from the wind. There was a second, unspoken reason, too. So no one else would see their lights as they dug through the winter night.

They fashioned the ice into a giant cube around the hand. As they dug underneath it, they propped it up with tyre jacks. It was all done with gusto but with very little regard for scientific fastidiousness. That's what got the results this far from anywhere: doggedness.

Muir was allowed to crawl under the block, her face inches from the ball of the mermaid's wrist bone. One cold and empty vein almost brushed her nose. She lay there while the cold crept into her parka. Vipond dragged her out by her ankles, laughing, pulling her to her feet. But only because it was his turn next.

When they released the hand from the ice, the next challenge was getting it back to Base. They had to use a Snow Cat, because winter winds had laid so much soft snow on the ground most of the other vehicles were stalled back at Base.

Even then they had to plot a course that wasn't the most direct way, but the way least likely to lose the cat into the underground.

They hooked up every towrope they had and dragged the cube, most people opting to walk alongside it. Everything was done in almost-silence and without any of the customary complaint. There was no sound except for the Snow Cat's grinding engine and the communal sounds of grunting and heaving.

The hand of the mermaid lay as still and supplicating as ever. The sides of the carved ice tank were so thick it was barely visible except from the top, but Muir would've sworn blind she saw one finger move, stretch, and retreat in its solid ice trailer.

That evening, she snuck the Otter out. Into the dark. No one tried to stop her. Half of them barely registered what was said to them anymore, and the others shivered not so much from cold but from an excess of nervous energy. Only the ice and darkness were still.

Muir flew with all lights on, her radio tuned to a standard station in case anyone else was out flying that night. When she crested the mermaid's ice cap, she tipped the plane so she could see right into her eyes, yellowed by the lights of her Otter. The itch, the fear, the nagging need that had been plaguing her, it was calmed.

The mermaid was there, always there. It hadn't been a hallucination or a dream. She was still trapped in her hard, white coffin, her icy face calm.

Muir had thought there might be some change in her expression as they dragged her stolen hand further away, towards Base. She was waiting for signs of life, waiting for her to turn her head and fix Muir with her eyes. Waiting for the mermaid to open her mouth and curse her. But she remained indifferent, held tight beneath the ice and the solid-black sky.

WHEN SHE GOT BACK, THEY'D CLEARED PART OF the hangar, wedging the resident vehicles against the walls or into other ports and apartments where they could. Some, in their haste, they banished to the elements outside.

Van der Zee, far away on Earth, had enough presence of mind to abuse them from the vid-link. He ranted about cost and damage. Concepts that had become unfamiliar to everyone left behind.

In the end they threw some tarps over the relocated vehicles to keep the worst of winter off. But they didn't move them back into the hangar. They needed the hangar.

Then they paused, Muir supposed, to think. The mermaid's hand was theirs now, but still sheathed in ice. As far removed as it had ever been. Muir heard them deliberating on whether to cut or burn it out. They tried both, using hand tools to first chip away. They creased the edges of the block, braiding it with their drills.

Ice fell and melted across the floor and was swept out with long brooms into the cold outside, where it froze on contact with the wind. A lip formed on the hangar entry.

Muir didn't like to watch, but still she couldn't leave. She was unnerved by Bayoumi's frozen concentration whenever she saw him, and the empty expressions on the faces of the others.

"You think she's real?" Partholon asked.

He'd stepped unbidden to Muir's side. Muir was outside the hangar's viewing windows, wind pressing her parka hood to her skull, hands plunged deep into pockets. She was jittering, and stomping her feet to drive the blood supply to her toes. The hangar lights lent Base an unearthly, orange light.

"Real?" Muir asked. "What do you mean?"

"You know." Partholon winked, as if he and Muir were the only ones in on the joke.

"No, I don't."

"They used to manufacture fake scientific discoveries. Back in the day. Furred fish and feathered, I don't know. Goats. So they could take these strange beasts back to courts and woo ladies. Or kings, see. Maybe the kings would give them more funding for expeditions."

"Right, I get it."

Partholon chuckled. "Wouldn't that be good, hey? A distraction from our missing wreck."

"There never was any kind of wreck, Partholon."

"So you say."

Muir sighed. "I wouldn't know anything about how to make something like this. I think she has to be real."

Partholon's voice was sharp, though his face was shadowed. "This can't be the only thing we find here, this stupid *whatever* it is."

"Maybe it is, maybe there's nothing else out there."

"Oh, there's something. They keep us here over winter. Can't do any scientific work, so why leave us here?"

"To keep Base running until summer," Muir reasoned. "Why are *you* here, Partholon?"

"I say management knows something's out there, they just don't know what. A wreck, something."

"Partholon." She reached out and spun him to face her. "There's no wreck."

"You think they really can't find one wreck on this little planet? If the damn thing's here, I bet they found it in the first half hour. And everything since has been one big fat lie to keep us busy and them"—he jerked his chin at the other rats in the hangar—"looking for whatever it is they're *really* looking for."

"Partholon, you're not making sense."

His eyes were wild and bloodshot, his face pinched.

Muir said, "You should go see Adriatico. She can give you something to help you sleep."

"You haven't asked me," Partholon said. "You haven't asked me what they're really looking for."

She sighed. "Okay, Partholon, what're they really looking for?"

Partholon leaned in as if to share a confidence. The hood of his parka engulfed hers, blocking out all light. He stank of stale alcohol and fish, and his breath brushed her face as he spoke.

"Aliens." He leaned back and smiled, the light from the window twisting his face into a hideous carnival mask. "For slaves."

Muir looked at him. "You're fucked up."

He frowned at her and sniggered, drawing his nostrils up in a snarl. She thought for a moment he might attack her. But he shook his head like he was clearing the sleep from his mind.

"Suit yourself," he said.

His face relaxed into a semblance of normality. Muir took a breath.

Vipond came up beside them. He looked from her to Partholon and back.

"Touching, isn't it?" he said.

"What is?"

She hoped he didn't mean her and Partholon.

"All those outsiders indoors together." He gestured through the hangar window. "The big, fat exo-indo."

He laughed. Vipond called the place Exonesia, his face crinkling into a grin every time he said it. Meaning: outworld. A place outside every other place.

"We're all outsiders here, hey?" Partholon had taken up the theme. "We're all escapees. Just stumbled across a new kind of prison, is all."

He nodded conspiratorially. Muir knew what was coming next.

"What're you in for, buddy?" Partholon whispered to her.

He'd tried every tone of voice he knew: friendly, warm, welcoming, demanding, insistent, violent. Muir remained immune. The goading wasn't worse than what her answer would have to be. *What're you in for, buddy?*

Vipond said, "Shut the hell up for once, Partholon."

Muir ignored them and kept her gaze trained on the hand of the mermaid. Inside they were making no discernible progress.

"A mermaid. Probably too much woman for you, though, eh, Muir?" Partholon sneered. "I hear you like 'em young. Little-girl young."

This wasn't unusual either, the sexual harassment, the trying-to-gauge-if-she-liked-men-or-women comments. But Partholon was tying it into something else.

Vipond began, "Partholon—"

Partholon said, "I hear you like them crushed under the wheels of your truck."

Muir wasn't big and she wasn't particularly strong, but she'd hated Partholon for a long time. She shot a fist towards his throat, right where the fur rim of his parka met in a V-shape. She punched him hard, once, then twice.

He gurgled and hacked, his eyes rolling in his head. He slumped against the hangar wall, one hand to his throat, gulping fish-mouthed and red.

For a moment Muir thought she might have killed him. Before her anger could give way to fear, she found herself wondering how long it would take anyone to notice. The mermaid had them. She'd taken them far away.

Partholon leaned against the wall, bent double over his knees. He hacked dramatically, hanging there while Muir thought about hitting him again. She'd thought it would leave her more ashamed, but it didn't. If anything, she was beginning to think this might become her new way of dealing with Partholon. She let the feeling blossom across her sternum. Bravado and hunger. She was glad for it, because it made every other feeling fade.

"Whoa," Vipond said.

He didn't move.

"Hello there!" Bayoumi crossed the snow towards them.

His parka was open, so maybe he'd seen them from inside and come for them. Muir stood by, willing to take whatever he was bringing. He stepped into the light from the window, and his face was split into high-contrast surrealism. He looked at Muir for a long time.

Then he turned to Partholon and reached for his head, hauling him upright. Partholon was still gulping and blinking. Bayoumi let him go, tapping his skull once against the wall behind him.

"No harm done," he observed.

"She attacked me!" Partholon gurgled.

"Somebody was going to. Eventually," Bayoumi replied.

He waved a gloved hand through the air.

That changed things for Partholon. For Muir, too, and probably Vipond. But for Partholon it was more immediate. He eased up straight at last and leaned against the wall.

His face was mottled purple and he was still retching. One hand he used to rub the ice from his eyes, where unspilled tears had frozen. The other hand he rested against the wall of the hangar, below the window where the scientists worked to free their artefact.

For one sweet, victorious moment Muir realised the mermaid didn't matter to her now. What mattered was that Partholon was looking at her with a newfound respect. Something that acknowledged the pure, angry power in her.

Bayoumi turned to Muir, sizing her up. "I would not have thought you had it in you."

Muir wanted to say, *I didn't*, because she probably hadn't had it in her. Not until now.

"You see what they're doing in there?" she asked.

His gaze drifted to the window. "They're not getting any closer."

"She wants her hand back, Bayoumi."

"Who does?"

"The... thing, in the ice. She wants her, what did you call it?"

"The ankh?" Bayoumi was thoughtful. "It was metres away from her. It was lost to her already."

"We shouldn't have brought it here," Muir said. "Now she's looking for it. Now she's found us."

Bayoumi's eyes were frosted. He was distant and lost.

"Damage has been done, Muir. We've cut it from the ice already."

"You think *that's* the damage?" Muir asked.

"What do you want us to do? Return it?"

"Exactly."

Bayoumi made no response. He gestured, his hands like wings. He looked at her like someone who was lost and didn't know it yet.

Muir said, "Can I take the Otter for a spin?"

Beside her, Vipond looked incredulous. "In the dark, in this weather?"

Muir figured she couldn't explain it, how the pulsing in her veins was louder, was singing to the mermaid in the ice. She figured even if she could get it into words that would make sense, it still wouldn't be believable.

She looked at Bayoumi, willing him to hear the siren call and feel the crazy stinging of the air. She wanted to ask him how he could breathe with the weight of this world's foreign atmosphere clinging and sticky like syrup.

She said, "Please?"

Beside her, Vipond was shaking his head. Partholon leaned almost forgotten against the wall, his eyes fixed on nothing.

"I have to draw the line," Bayoumi said, his broad face pulling back from the light. "Van der Zee would never forgive me if something happened to you."

"I'm not his pet."

Bayoumi shrugged. "Regardless."

He left and Muir watched him go. She realised from the blur of his receding back that it had started snowing.

Vipond leaned forward. He grabbed Partholon by the lapel of his parka and gave him another gentle shove into the wall.

"Partholon, you've been begging for someone to realign your attitude since we got here," he said.

"Ouch," Partholon replied.

The three of them stood there, like they were waiting for something. Partholon leaned his head to the window, where the hangar's thick light hung in the air.

"There should be a punch line," he said.

"To what?" Vipond asked.

"All this."

Partholon flung out his arms wide, a kind of mimicry of Bayoumi's more delicate, quiet gestures. Muir chuckled. Vipond joined her, though his laugh was loose and uncertain. She figured Partholon was the punch line and he just didn't realise. It made her feel invincible.

"What's so funny?" Partholon asked.

That made her laugh harder. Partholon straightened with an expletive. He pulled free of the wall, jerking upright. His parka ripped, leaving an orange nylon stain in the weak light under the window.

"What the hell?" he muttered, his voice hoarse.

He buffed the wall with the side of his hand, sending nylon dandruff into the air. Like the scientist he was, he pressed his palm to the wall and stood like he was waiting for something. Then suddenly he jerked back, pulling his hand free as if he'd been stung.

"Jesus," he croaked. "I'm burning. My hand's burning."

Muir grabbed for his fingers. The glove had ripped away and his palm was exposed and red-raw, blue along the sides of his fingers.

Vipond asked, "Frostbite?"

Partholon shook Muir off. "Like I stuck my hand in liquid nitrogen. Jesus!"

He rubbed at the raw mess of his palm. Soft pink dust rose into the air to meet the snow.

"Well, don't do that, then," Vipond muttered.

Muir pressed a fingertip to the remnants of Partholon's glove on the wall. She felt an icy blast sting her finger and she drew back sharply.

"This is not good," Partholon muttered.

Inside the hangar, something else had changed. The scientists had gone from their determined movements around the artefact to a series of stomping and arm-slapping. Like they were cold, Muir thought. Worse than cold. Like they were freezing.

"Hey," called one of the rats, "someone turn the goddamned heat up in here!"

"Whole place is freezing since they brought her here," Partholon muttered outside. "Whole goddamn place."

He was right. Muir was so used to shivering she hardly noticed it anymore. The cold lived in her cheeks, in her nose, under her eyes. It made her ears ache and added a thick numbness to her tongue and limbs. More than anything, the cold had always made her feel dumb and slow.

But now, as Partholon slunk into the dark towards the infirmary, she didn't feel that at all. She felt like the shivering was all that was keeping her alive. It was her whole being.

As the saws neared the mermaid's milky skin, her shivering increased. They were all shivering, everyone, even inside, even the ones wearing their parkas in the hangar. Everyone was.

"I'm getting out of here," Muir said.

Vipond grunted. "And going where?"

But Muir knew where.

It was the middle of the night, but it would be the middle of the night for six more months. Muir's Otter was outside the hangar, stacked side by side with Waterman's Spryte and an old Cat with a rubbish-run cage on the back, used to haul garbage.

The snow crunched under her as she crouched to pull the stocks from under the Otter's wheels.

"What do you think you're doing?" Waterman was behind her, clipboard in hand.

Even in the midst of all the craziness, some people were still trying to keep to the old standards. In this place, that had become the primal urge; the need for structure, for an almost forgotten discipline.

"Need to check on something," Muir said. "Van der Zee's direct order."

Waterman frowned. "Van der Zee's giving orders?"

"He's always given the orders. He's in charge."

Waterman spat. "I mean, remotely?"

"Bayoumi passed it on," Muir improvised. She got to her feet. "Hey, Waterman, what did you see? In the ice?"

"This again." Waterman rested against her Spryte. "I saw a good old-fashioned Star of David. Still seeing a mermaid?"

"Yeah."

"Does that mean you worship weird, occult shit?"

"I don't worship anything," Muir replied.

"Probably why you got stuck with a mutant fish," Waterman grunted.

"Okay."

"You should find something to believe in, Muir. Before it's too late."

"Too late for what?"

Waterman didn't have an answer. Instead she asked, "You're a winter-over now, right?"

"Guess so."

"So, what, no funeral?"

"Guess not." Muir tried to stay calm.

"Your mother's where? Still on ice?"

Something wrenched behind Muir's ribs. Like someone had plunged a knife into her lungs.

"She's not on ice," Muir said. "She's dead. She's gone. She doesn't care about some damn funeral, do you understand? She's immune to me now."

"Immune to you?" Waterman said. "What's that mean?"

Muir wanted to say, *She can't be hurt by me anymore.* She realised for the first time that what she felt about her mother was relief. Her mother was free from the reach—the kick, the punch—of life. Free from the cold, sharp shock of life. And Muir envied her.

She ducked under the wing and looked at Waterman from the other side of it. "Help me move this damn thing."

"And let you destroy thousands of dollars of aircraft?" Waterman shook her head. "Not even if it'll knock some sense into you. I'm getting the hangar manager."

"If de Marinis had a problem with someone using the Otters, he wouldn't have given permission to store them outside."

"De Marinis is crazy, like the rest of them."

"And you're not?"

Waterman ignored her. In the chaos of what was happening to Base, she was amazed to think Waterman thought *she* was the crazy one. She looked around at the freezing hangar, at the people who worked their frozen vision free—hand, ankh, whatever the hell they thought it was. She realised their movements were methodical, concerted. Not shivering anymore.

And she wondered if Waterman was right. Maybe she was crazy. Maybe everyone else was sane.

But she also knew something else. They would never get that thing free of its ice casing. They would never free it because they could never touch the edges of something that existed as much in their imaginations as it did anywhere else.

She worked the Otter forward, first pushing at one wing and then scooting low under the belly to shove at the other. No one stopped her. Vipond passed and she stepped back into the shadows. He had an expression like he was lost, or dreaming. But then he turned back to the mystery in the hangar and the drills and the heat and noise, and she was free.

Muir leapt into the Otter and started it, letting the engine whine and scream until she could feel some warmth through the dashboard. The lights were useless in the heavy dark, turning the black haze grey for about half a metre in front of her. Useless for visibility, but she hoped they'd at least warn anyone between her and the sky that she was coming.

The Otters were chosen for their short take-offs. She made use of that now, rolling forward barely two metres before rising, battered by snow, into the air. But now the air was as heavy as the earth, and it weighed her down. It was like moving through seawater.

No one had ever asked Muir what her mother did. She existed simply as a death for them, not as a human being. If she'd ever done anything, it was assumed that was long ago and a long way away. Muir's mother had been a farmer. An ocean farmer. Seaweed and, when that fell out of fashion, red sea bream. She'd been good at it, too. She had loved poetry though her daughter hated it. Had talked about the old ways but never with compulsion, always with joy. Had loved her daughter. Had even found a way to forgive her.

Her mother—her okaasan, in the Earth language—had been called Amaya Kaito, and she had named her daughter Fuyuko. It meant 'child of winter'. She'd given Fuyuko her father's name, Muir, though he was already dead. Child of winter, child of sea. Had cursed her with that name, though that probably wasn't her intention.

Muir flew, by instinct, into the slant of the snow. The torrents of wind held her back, and the snow. And her own fear of what she would find. She followed the coordinates on her dashboard. No voice interrupted to ask what she was doing. No one was watching back at Base.

Blindly, not realising it at first, Muir flew straight out over the ice cap where the mermaid lay. In the misleading snow, she landed so close to an unnamed ridge that her right wing shuddered and the metal in the Otter's belly sang with reverberation. She scooted to a stop with the Otter's nose aimed at the mermaid's face, her wheels on the mermaid's hair, the weak plane lights finding the highlights in her eyes and chin and collarbones. Lighting up the bones beneath the mermaid's icy skin.

Muir imagined she even breathed.

She got out of the Otter and for the first time realised she was warm. Following one twisted tangle of the mermaid's hair, she thought she might lie beside the mermaid's wide lips or curl into the shell of her ear.

Suddenly the ice cap gave way beneath her.

She fell, pitching forward, following her misplaced foot. She slammed her elbow on the ice and also her forehead and one shoulder. She grasped for something to stop her descent, but there was nothing.

Around her the ice cracked in tiny explosions. Her back arched as she fell knee first, trying to twist like a fish on a line. Turning her face away from the freezing draught just in time to take the blow of her fall along her shoulder and torso instead of her skull.

The ice shelf knocked the wind out of her. Wrenched it out of her. She felt her ribs squelch. Something snapped in her arm. Her jaw hit, slamming teeth into teeth. She rolled onto her back, trying to find her breath.

Above her, the Otter fell in a shower of snow. It pitched towards where Muir lay and broke its propeller on the cruel ice edge. Then it hung by its wings, swinging, snow scattering from its wheels.

Its weak light illuminated the mermaid and then the cave where Muir had fallen. As it rocked, the mermaid glittered and danced beside and above her, the smooth lines of her body flickering. The snow fell around Muir like static.

She didn't hurt yet. Every part of her body that had hit or slammed or crunched now shook. A vacuum had replaced her elbow through to her shoulder, and a strange, crawling sensation like insects was attacking her chin and jaw. But in the quiet, away from the chaos and smell of Base, she felt for the first time a kind of peace. A conditional peace, something fragile.

Her eyes stung but she wouldn't cry; she'd been too long in this place to think of crying as anything but dangerous. Even when her mother died, she hadn't cried. And if Muir were to die here, she wanted to die not with her eyes wedged open by frozen tears, cruelly staring up at the serene form of the mermaid. The goddess. The water demon. The Ningyo, whose flesh offered immortality but whose presence harbinged tragedy. Ningyo, with its human face and monstrous fish-body. Its tiny teeth.

"Too late," Muir whispered.

If the Ningyo intended to warn her that her mother was dead or that Muir herself was dying, it was too late for all that.

She thought the stories had done Ningyo a disservice, though. She wasn't a hideous fish, she was beautiful, the glittering mermaid above her.

A ringing pain was starting down her right side. Her head thudded and pulsed. Her eyes stung. She burned and she hurt and every breath reignited the red pain along her side.

She gagged. She turned to the side and hacked bloody phlegm into the ice at her shoulder.

The mermaid writhed in the snowy haze offered by the Otter's failing light. Muir lay under that massive monster, watching it slither in and out of focus, meeting its cold gaze. She realised she was ready to die. She'd been ready a long time.

They found her. She didn't know how they did it. But they found her. It took hours. The throbbing pain in her arm and side was almost tolerable. It had become familiar. Her fingers and toes had done burning. Now they were numb.

The lights from the Otter had failed at last. Muir lay in darkness.

Waterman called from the ice above her but she refused to answer. So they shone torches into her tomb and shouted when they found her. Muir lay still. The torchlight turned her eyelids into red paisley swirls.

Waterman was shouting, a high urgency plaiting her voice. Muir could hear them snaking ropes down into the gap where she lay, the hiss of the fibre coils unspooling and snapping as they hit the icy floor. Muir turned her head to watch. She could hear Waterman's shout of relief, heralding her return to the land of the living.

Waterman rappelled down the ropes towards her. Muir shut her eyes against the onslaught of humanity.

"Jesus, Muir, what the hell happened?" Waterman said.

"I fell."

"Bayoumi's ready to kill you."

"Let him."

Waterman laughed, mistaking her meaning. "That's the spirit. You've got your mermaid to thank for us even finding you."

"What do you mean?"

"I mean she lit up against the clouds. I guess when the Otter tried to follow you in."

"You saw her?" Muir asked.

"Don't ask me how. Took some fancy driving to get here, I can tell you." She gave Muir a sidelong look.

"You saw her, the mermaid?"

"I saw your freaking mermaid, I told you. As bright as Christmas. Everybody saw her."

Muir didn't believe it. The dim Otter lights wouldn't have been enough, the mermaid wouldn't have been visible to the people who'd seen Egyptian goddesses and crucifixes and Stars of David and lotus flowers, and all the many things that had been claimed.

She said, "Are you sure you saw a *mermaid*?"

"It's not a competition, Muir," Waterman grimaced. "Don't be so damn glad your oversized fish won out."

But Muir was glad. Finally the tears began to form, and she had to brush them away with her uninjured arm, her fingers barely extending beyond the parka's sleeve.

"Can you feel it, Waterman?" she asked. "Out here, away from the drills and the need to get that thing out of the ice. It's sane out here."

Waterman's expression shifted, and Muir knew she could feel it. *It's not just me*, Muir thought, and was glad.

Some latent fellow-feeling welled inside her and she gripped Waterman's hand. Waterman seemed surprised, even stilled. She looked like she was afraid to move her hand from Muir's but uncertain how to leave it there. In the end she squeezed Muir's fingers and placed her hand back on top of her parka.

Waterman took refuge in the practical details of Muir's recovery.

"Frostbite's going to be a problem," she muttered. "Out of the wind, so maybe not so bad. Although, how the hell you managed to get in here..."

She shone her torch around the ice walls, apparently examining them for signs of Muir's survival. The light of the torch lit up something brilliant and golden. As if the sun, when it set, had set here in one wall beneath the mermaid.

Muir was dazzled by it. She blinked against the brightness. Beside her, Waterman's low laugh began deep in her throat.

"Hey," she shouted to the others still above the ice. "Hey, someone! Tell Partholon. We found his goddamn ducks."

Muir blinked as a hundred entombed yellow ducks came into focus, lining the inner wall.

THEY WRAPPED HER IN SILVER THERMA-SHEETING and dragged her up on a makeshift gurney, tying the ends of a tarp around her. They hoisted her through the tomb's roof, past the mermaid's forehead.

Muir wanted to stay, every fibre of her body aching for the relief the mermaid promised. She was sorry she'd ever compared the mermaid to Ningyo, sorry she couldn't find a way to convince them to let her stay. Sorry when her fingers began to ache and burn in the back of the Snow Cat, where they laid her.

Her head rested on Vipond's lap as Adriatico leaned over to take her temperature and pulse and remove her gloves to feel her fingers.

"She's cold," Adriatico announced. "Freezing cold."

"Great diagnosis, Medici," Vipond muttered. "You're worth your weight in rubber ducks."

Adriatico grunted.

Vipond pulled the therma-sheet further up, covering Muir's ears.

It crackled like fire, like an ocean breaking. She pitched and rolled with the Cat as it made its way back to Base. Waterman was on the phone for the whole drive, talking to Bayoumi.

"She's fine," Waterman said.

She didn't mention the potential frostbite, Muir noticed.

"And the plane?" Bayoumi's voice from the radio.

"It's... maybe recoverable."

A long silence from the radio. Then Bayoumi asked, "How'd she get out there?"

Waterman hesitated. "Can't keep a good pilot down."

"Van der Zee will have someone's hide for this. Mine, probably."

"He can have mine, sir," Waterman said with unaccustomed politeness. She clicked off the radio. "He can have it. Whatever the hell that's worth in today's market."

"Sir," Muir croaked.

"What'd she say?" Waterman asked.

"I think she just called me sir," Vipond replied.

Waterman let out a short laugh. Adriatico wrapped her bare hand across Muir's forehead, warming her. Vipond held her close. Vipond, crossing by land, not air, obeying the command not to fly.

"You're a good man, Vipond," she said.

"I know it."

Vipond, for the longest time, her only friend on the Base. She wondered what he thought of her now.

Above and around them the sky was dark, the Otter's lights failing to light up the mermaid against the sky. Leaving her to lie in the dark. Broken in the ice.

"So what's with the suicide attempt?" Vipond asked.

She tried to laugh. Vipond was serious, though, his dark eyes still as a frozen ocean. Muir shrugged and didn't try to correct him. There was no reason. She could feel the end of the world coming.

"You need me?" Waterman asked.

She was all puffed up with pride at her successful rescue in the dark.

"No," Adriatico replied.

"Good," Waterman said, too loudly. "Bayoumi wants me on his call to Van der Zee. You could be in big trouble, Muir."

Muir shrugged. Her fingers had stopped aching, but three of them were blackened and hard at the tips. She waved Waterman off with those fingers and saw Waterman's face change.

"Take good care of our girl, Medici," Waterman said.

"Always," Adriatico replied.

Vipond carried her to the infirmary and—at Adriatico's orders—deposited her on a gurney, where she slouched while Adriatico fussed.

"You too, Vipond, out," Adriatico said.

"If you need me," Vipond began, his gaze searching.

"For what?" Muir asked.

Vipond left, his expression unreadable. Muir lay back on the hard gurney, waiting for Adriatico's useless ministrations.

"Are they still trying to get to the artefact?" she asked.

"The rats? Oh, yeah."

"Think they'll want to investigate the church now?"

"The church? What church?" Adriatico frowned.

"What do they call," Muir took a breath, "the place where they found me?"

"That was a hole in the ground," Adriatico muttered. "With ducks. You call that a church? That's weird, Muir."

The infirmary was the quietest place on Base. There was no conversation, no motors, no generators or pistons, no Snow Cats or Sprytes or Otters.

"What's your secret?" Muir asked.

"My secret what?"

Muir changed tack. "How are you not affected?"

She stumbled over the last word.

"Affected?" Adriatico smiled. "Or infected?"

Adriatico had hazel eyes and tawny skin that was still pale enough to be sunburned out here in the snow.

"Either."

"I'm always an outsider," Adriatico shrugged.

"Most of us are," Muir replied.

"Yeah, well," Adriatico shuffled through a drawer, pulling out warming pads and activating them with a slap on the bench. "I'm even an outsider to the outsiders."

She pressed the pads to Muir's chest and head. She took Muir's temperature with a thermometer in her ear. She grunted at the result and felt for a pulse at her neck. Adriatico worked on Muir as if she wasn't there.

"You've never called me Medici," she said suddenly.

"It's a stupid nickname," Muir replied.

"Why?"

"The Medici family were patrons of art and architecture. Not medicine."

Adriatico turned wide eyes on her. "You been reading up on Italian history?"

"I have an interest," Muir said.

Adriatico moved to a sink and started pouring hot water into a basin. "It has them, you know."

"What does?"

"Whatever it is you found in the ice, *amica*." She effected the accent, perfected with practice.

"Listen, Adriatico." Muir struggled to sit upright. "What do you see, when you look at it?"

Adriatico shrugged. "I'm Catholic."

"So?"

"So I see our Saviour nailed to a crucifix."

"And?"

Adriatico stripped off Muir's heavy white boots and thick socks. She plunged Muir's feet into the basin, bending her knees up. A current of pain ran through Muir's toes. Adriatico wrapped her hands with warm bandages that burned like fire. Then she pushed her back down onto the gurney.

"And, what?" she prompted.

"And, you don't feel anything about that? Any... fear or surprise or...? I don't know. Comfort?"

"Why should I be surprised?" Adriatico took a seat by the gurney. "God is everywhere. Even distant worlds, even places like this that everyone else wants to see as godforsaken."

"Nice."

"There are no forsaken places in all of existence," Adriatico replied, her voice taking on the quiet fervour of the believer.

"That simple, huh?" Muir asked.

"It is when you believe," Adriatico replied. "But before you believe, nothing is simple."

Muir glanced away, at the ceiling and the walls and all the glinting, ordered medical things in the room.

"I don't believe," she said.

"Not in anything?"

"Not in anything I know of."

"And so you see mermaids." Adriatico smiled. "And you get treated for frostbite. While I order hot water from the kitchen and know that tomorrow I'll still be able to hold a fork with my own, undamaged hands. I'll have to take some of your fingers off."

"All of them?"

"Three. The tips. Below the nail, probably," Adriatico said. "So. You hungry?"

Muir reeled. "Wow, that's cold, Adriatico. I mean…Sorry. Poor choice of words."

Adriatico laughed and she joined in, despite herself.

That was why Adriatico was unpopular at Base. Her lack of anxiety, her apparent lack of compassion. Her assurance that everything ended well, even life. Especially life, which ended in the arms of a mysterious and caring being just on the other side of the mortal veil.

"Why'd you go into medicine, Adriatico? Instead of, I don't know, architecture."

"Why'd you try to kill yourself, Muir?"

"I fell."

Adriatico smiled. "Me too."

Adriatico came back later to tell her Van der Zee had requested emergency medivac for her from Base.

"But no one can fly in the dark," Muir said. "And besides, it's against regulations."

Van der Zee's most ardent love. Regulations.

"Regulations aren't worth a damn when they're worried about lawsuits," he replied. "Suicide doesn't look good on a company's records."

"I'd be dead, how could I sue anyone?"

"Your family—"

"All beat me to it," she said. "Dead."

Adriatico shrugged. "I dunno, Vipond might sue."

"What's that mean?"

"It means Van der Zee's not taking any chances. He'll find a way to get you out."

When Muir didn't reply, she reached out and squeezed her hand. The undamaged one.

"You're going home, Muir. And about time, too, if you ask me."

"I didn't."

Adriatico smiled and squeezed harder, but Muir could barely feel it. Something worse than frostbite was numbing her.

Adriatico told her not to worry, to stay put and wait. But she couldn't.

She made her way to the hangar door, one hand bandaged like large white larvae. Muir's hospital gown was thin under the red parka she'd lifted from the infirmary. She moved further into the hangar, out of the wind. The space was oddly unfamiliar without its customary Otters.

Inside, people sagged over their work, taking aim at the thing in the ice with drill and flame. They'd moved on to power tools, and there was a generator hooked up intravenously to the machines.

They had worked open a split in the frozen mass. The white skin of the mermaid's thumb was visible like bone in a wound. The rats swore they could see her pores.

"They got through," Muir said out loud.

No one answered. The sight of success in the ice made them frantic.

The more they worked, the colder it seemed to get inside the hangar. Most were blaming the chunks of frozen ocean they were sawing away. The rest superstitiously raised totems and other items from forgotten religions. None of them asked for the work to stop. If anything, the freezing temperature seemed to improve their want. Muir could feel it, too.

Partholon was there, face blank with concentration. He'd taken on the job of sweeping the fallen ice shards. Where he'd carted them outside they sat in mounds like a blank graveyard. Muir found a broom and began helping. He didn't acknowledge her. His gaze was turned inward.

She stayed up through the night and into the dark morning, and so did everyone. Vipond kept her company, more often than not. Through the dark, cold hours where the seams between day and night had lost all sense.

They stood outside the fringe of rats hard at work on the mermaid's hand. They stole cups of coffee from the galley to warm their hands. They took turns wiping the windows to keep open a gap in the frost.

They traded stories of their lives, hesitantly at first. Vipond was the youngest of six. His mother had supported them after their father had left. She'd died young, Vipond barely remembered her.

"You should go to your mother's funeral," he said.

"Yeah."

"Medici says your medivac flight will be here in," he checked his watch, "eight hours."

"Great."

There were always rats in the hangar, red-eyed with lack of sleep, working with whatever tools were at hand. They lived in their suits now. Worked, ate, even slept. Thermostats were set to maximum, heaters were attached to the generator in the hangar. The temperature continued to fall. Bayoumi ordered techs to investigate. They found nothing.

"Don't you know?" Muir asked him. "It's her."

"Her?" Bayoumi asked.

"The mermaid."

He looked at her. "Shouldn't you be in the infirmary?"

"Maybe that's why the oceans were frozen. Maybe she brought down this whole world with cold."

Bayoumi chuckled. "Stick to piloting, Muir. Science tells us this place is frozen because it's so far from a sun."

But Muir couldn't let it go. She was onto something.

"Maybe she was lost, abandoned by her ancestors," she said. "Or maybe they had to get rid of her. To survive."

The way we *should get rid of her*, she wanted to add. The way she's clouding our minds, freezing our bodies.

Bayoumi only smiled.

"Maybe, Muir. Maybe." He made to leave. "You should return to the infirmary. Van der Zee would say, that's an order."

Muir had no intention of following the second-hand order. She stayed where she was, but Bayoumi must have called Adriatico. She was there moments later, taking firm hold of Muir's elbow.

"I'm in trouble for letting you out," Adriatico said. "Apparently you're raving like a crazy person."

"*I'm* crazy? Look at this."

She gestured around the hangar, where people were stomping their feet and slapping their upper arms, trying to force the freezing blood around their bodies. Eyebrows and beards—for those who had beards—were icy, faces pinched. And everyone had that same narrow stare.

"Maybe she was dumped here on purpose," Muir persisted. "Maybe she's a Trojan horse?"

"Hey. Maybe," Adriatico said.

Muir thought she was being teased, but when she looked at Adriatico's face, she seemed serious.

"You think this is all due to her, too. Don't you?" Muir asked. "All the cold and the weirdness. You think it's her?"

"It's something," Adriatico agreed. "I've half a mind to get on that medivac flight with you, if I'm honest."

Most winter-overs stayed because they had no place else to go. The mermaid had changed that.

Muir rubbed at the frostbite on her good hand, wincing as the mottled white-and-purple skin was pressed through clear thermagloves.

Adriatico's gaze tracked the hangar over Muir's shoulder, giving Muir notice of someone else's arrival. From her wide, wishful stare, Muir guessed it was Nerissa Dylan. A junior rat who wanted to be a senior rat. She had dark-red hair and pale-green eyes.

"What is it about her, hey?" Muir asked.

Adriatico chuckled. "What is it about you and Vipond?"

"What about nothing."

"I won't tell if you won't, Muir."

"Who am I gonna tell? I'm leaving in six hours."

"Oh, yeah. About that," Adriatico said. "Medivac's been delayed. Ice storm in the atmosphere. They're waiting for it to die down."

Muir felt the release of something from her sternum. "How long?"

"Hours, days. They'll let us know." Adriatico's gaze was lost again. "A stay of execution."

Vipond moved towards them, eyes narrowed. He leaned a shoulder against the wall, wrapping his arms around himself, his dark skin silvered by the cold and the snow.

"Something's wrong," he said without preliminaries. He was shivering and his voice was slurred, coming from between frozen lips. "I know you both feel it. And even if you can't feel it, surely you can see it?"

"Of course," said Adriatico. "The cold."

Vipond said, "With the amount of fuel we're using, we should be getting better heat than this. We must be into reserves by now."

"Well into, I'd guess," Muir replied. "When they dumped us here, they planned to use power from the glacial rivers."

"What glacial rivers?" Adriatico asked.

"Exactly."

Vipond shook his head. "I don't think Bayoumi understands the severity—"

"He's as mad as the rest of them," Adriatico cut him off.

Muir wanted to ask, *And we're not?* But Vipond was already rushing on.

"Why the change of heart, Vipond?" Muir asked. "I've seen you sweeping up the shavings like a good foot when Partholon's away."

"I dunno, I don't feel right," Vipond said. "I feel bad."

"You don't look right, either," Adriatico replied. "We should probably get you to the infirmary."

"And do what, Medici?" Vipond snapped. His eyes shifted uncomfortably. "They can do what they want here, but I'm getting the hell to Base Station Deux. With or without Bayoumi's approval."

"That's on the other side of the planet," Muir said. "You might as well say you'll medivac home with me."

"When's the plane arrive?" Something stirred in Vipond's dark eyes.

Muir shrugged. "Days."

"Wasn't that meant to happen already?"

"Storm," Adriatico told him.

"Whatever." Vipond shook off the news. "I'll tell Bayoumi I have to get home. They can keep their crazy mermaid. All I need is an Otter."

"You'll never make it in an Otter."

"I'll steal Waterman's favourite Cat, then. For God's sake," he said, "even our suits can't take this cold. My damn boots are too stiff to walk in. If we don't get out of here, we'll die."

He stepped away from the wall, and his suit gave a crackling noise as it pulled clear of the ice.

On the white pouching of the wall's insulation, ice was patterned like feathers, like needles and narrow blades and the jagged white edges of waves. As if Base was splintering from the inside out. A frozen explosion. It reminded Muir of Partholon just a day earlier, leaning against the outside of the hangar. But this wall was inside. It shouldn't be so cold *inside*.

"You okay?" she asked.

"It's freezing, Base is freezing." Vipond inspected the wall.

Adriatico said, "If this keeps up, the systems will shut down. And if we're out of heat and power, we'll shut down, too."

"And if we're still inside when that happens—" Muir began.

"Inside will be about as much good as outside," Adriatico concluded.

Matter-of-fact, like always.

Muir's imagination rushed her with images of the Base Station, frozen into perfect stillness alongside the hand of the mermaid. That's how they'd be found, by the next crew, the next miners and explorers. The next pilot, like her, roaming wide of her boundaries, looking for something. Following whatever called her.

"We'll be entombed," she said, "with that damn monster's hand."

Vipond looked at her. Or not quite at her. Past her. "First time you've called your precious mermaid a monster."

"Delusion's wearing off," Adriatico murmured. "It doesn't need our minds anymore. It's got our bodies."

"You really think that?" Vipond asked.

"No," said Adriatico. "Because I think what it's after is our souls."

Between them, Muir felt redundant. She guessed that's what kept Bayoumi frozen too, what kept them all here trying to out-wait each other. She wanted to argue, to talk about the cultural importance of what they'd found, the scientific impact of whatever it was they were going through. Not about souls or mind-eaters.

But logic was a rat's job and the roles weren't clear anymore.

She turned away from the wall, back to the activity around the frozen hand. And for the first time, the hand seemed to have gone. All that remained was the ice.

"My God," she whispered. "Do you see that?"

"What?" Adriatico asked.

Muir turned to her. "There's nothing in the ice."

THE SOUNDS OF DRILLS SCREAMED ON AND ON, but something in the hangar had changed.

Everywhere the rats were still. Hands holding instruments were frozen in the air, though saws continued to burr and roll. In the rare gaps in thermal suiting, skin and eyes were as white and clear as snow.

Muir said, "We need to get out. Right now."

"And go where?" Adriatico asked.

Muir grabbed her hand and went to push Vipond ahead of her.

"What…" Vipond said, his words thickening in the numbing cold. "What's going on?"

Muir pushed but Vipond seemed stuck. He was turning slowly to face them, and his skin was rime-white from his collar to his whitened hair. His eyes had dulled to a dirty dark marble. When he opened his mouth to speak, a puff of ice-cold air frosted in front of him.

Muir watched as ice crawled up his throat and froze his tongue. It turned his face to crystal from the inside out.

"Jesus." A tingle of cold air brushed Muir's nose and she reeled back. "Run. Run!"

They did. They lurched around Vipond's frozen figure and ran. Randomly.

"Get out!" Muir screamed at the rats.

No one moved.

"They're gone, Muir," Adriatico shouted. "They're dead already."

Adriatico ran ahead, dragging Muir behind. They raced from the hangar mouth, back around to the corridor that connected them to the rest of Base.

Maybe there was warmth further in. Maybe they'd find a pocket of it. Muir imagined fingers of ice reaching between her shoulder blades.

The corridors were a blur of grey nano-sheeting. The windows pressed against a thick ice storm that enclosed Base Station Un like a gullet.

Across the soft insulated flooring their footsteps didn't even echo. Maybe they were ghosts already.

Adriatico fell away and Muir turned, thinking she'd stumbled. But Adriatico had found a door and beside it an emergency alarm. She leapt to it, trying to smash the glass with the side of her fist. There was a rime of ice across it. Unbreakable, unbendable, stronger than the glass it protected.

"Step back," Muir said.

She grabbed the axe set into the wall above the alarm and hammered at the glass. Her shoulders jarred and trembled as she fought with the ice. A tearing shriek and the glass caved at last.

Adriatico reached for the lever inside and twisted. The ululating wail of the alarm echoed through Base and out, into the dark.

The thickest exosuits, the ones too impractical to wear while drilling or manoeuvring, lay in a pile by the door. Refugees from the clearance of the hangar. Muir struggled into one, pulling the stiff suit up over her other layers of clothes. One more defence against the cold.

Adriatico followed her lead but she looked confused. She was probably wondering whether Muir really thought they could beat this thing. Whatever it was.

For Muir, that had stopped mattering. She was working automatically, the animal part of her brain determined to survive.

They heard running and shouts in the corridors. It was Waterman, fully clothed but blinking from sleep, her hair a mess.

"Muir? The hell? What's with the alarm?"

"Get out," Muir told her. "Base is ruptured."

"Sweet Mother of…"

Waterman took the rest of the corridor at full sprint. Hopefully towards her Spryte. She didn't even stop for a suit. Waterman was tough, but Muir wondered crazily how far she thought she could get in cold like this.

Others ran past, but randomly, directionless. Muir yelled at all of them to get out, get suited, get shelter.

Her bandaged hand was too big to get through the sleeve.

"Adriatico?"

The doctor hesitated. Then she zipped up her own suit and leaned into Muir's sleeve. She pulled the bandage out like a snake charmer uncoiling a python.

"Try not to bang it," she told Muir.

Muir slapped the seals shut, ignoring her foreshortened fingertips under plaster.

The exo-suit did nothing to raise her temperature, even when she dialled up the gas in the membranes. It was like hoping a photo of a fireplace could warm her feet.

She pulled up the hood, and they followed Waterman's direction along the corridor.

They reached the edge of Base without finding her.

"Ready?" Muir asked.

Adriatico nodded.

Muir punched at a door control and they stepped into the white-dark of the ice storm.

She could feel the cold deep in the meat of her body. She felt the pinch of iciness between brows, across toes, along the insides of her thighs. All the tenderest places. Her eyes were painful with arid winds. Every breath pulled in more of the cold, but the air didn't seem to reach her lungs.

The radio headpiece sat awkwardly against her ear. She hadn't taken the time to fit it right. Already the buzz of conversation vibrated against her ear lobe. Distant, hard to make out.

"Can you hear me?" she said. "Can anyone hear me? Acknowledge."

Adriatico was heading back towards the outside of the hangar doors, bowed under the weight of the storm. Muir figured she was aiming for one of the Snow Cats sitting under tarps in the layering snow. There was no sign of Waterman anywhere.

Muir set out after Adriatico, leaning heavily on the exterior walls of Base. There was a strange chiming sound in her ear, and she realised it was the suit. Some kind of auditory status report on the suit's condition. She had no idea what the notes meant. She realised she was limping and hoped it wasn't frostbite, not so soon.

The wind swept into her face. Her vision was liquid grey at the edges. Stress, she thought. Or snow. She wiped at her eyes. She didn't need to see, so long as she could keep a hand on the wall.

"Adriatico?" she called. "Waterman?"

No answer. She didn't know who was left inside. Hippocratic oath be damned, Adriatico hadn't checked, either. Muir understood it. Self-preservation, the will to survive. The only thing left, the only reason she was here, outside and upright, and not lying on a cold floor sucking ice into her throat.

In a brief respite from the wind, she spied Adriatico ahead of her. She was gesturing to a parked snowplough under its tarpaulin tent. Muir gave her a thumbs-up and Adriatico gestured to the driver's side. Muir reached out and grabbed her shoulder.

"It's too slow," she shouted into Adriatico's parka. "We'll never get away."

"To move the ice," Adriatico shouted back.

Muir realised suddenly. Adriatico didn't want to escape, she wanted to move the mermaid's hand away from Base. Back, into the ice.

She ran for the plough, both legs numb to the knees. She climbed in stiffly and pulled the door closed after her.

In the small, sealed cabin, she was at least safe from the wind. The tremble in her hands wasn't obvious through the thick gloves. But she could feel it.

She started the plough and spun it on its thick wheels, aiming for the hangar.

Adriatico ran ahead.

Inside, the stillness was mesmerising, the frozen rats lit up and glittering with ice. From this distance Muir couldn't tell if the saws were still working, held in their frozen hands.

Between her and the slab of ice were three rats, frozen, milk dust across faces that were as blank as slate. Adriatico was trying to shift them, but her movements were slowing and the rats weren't budging.

Muir angled the plough into the hangar and waited for Adriatico to back away. She nudged the frozen rats, gently at first. Trying to gather them up. But with a lurch the plough shoved harder and the rats fell.

They shattered noiselessly to grey ash, and the tools they held scattered.

Muir hadn't known grief could be so silent. She didn't want to watch, but she couldn't bear their deaths to go unwitnessed. She dared herself to look into each face as it disintegrated. Then she pushed her way through the hangar.

She travelled to the far side of the ice. As she turned the plough, she nicked the left leg of a rat and watched him half-spin and tip, almost like he was dancing. It was Bayoumi. There was an expression of sad realisation on his face, and a broad, rough longing.

Then he fell and splintered against the ground, scattering across the floor all the way to where Vipond stood with his frozen back to Muir's assault. She figured if she got out of this, she'd come back for Vippond. She'd bury him in the snow. She'd bury them all if she could.

The Base alarm sounded a dull, bleating eulogy, barely penetrating the thick cabin of the plough. Muir could hear the chimes of her suit change until they sounded like a distress signal. She ignored it.

Something was shifting in the middle of the slab of white ice. It jerked once as it connected with the plough.

She nearly dropped it as she headed back to the hangar doors. Frostbite, she realised. Her arms and legs were progressively numb. She couldn't tell if she was connecting with the controls unless she watched her hands.

She had no idea where Adriatico had gone. She only hoped the doctor wasn't between her and the doors.

She gritted her teeth and kept moving. There was just her now, and this icy, dying world. They belonged together.

She pushed past the edge of the hangar and into the dark, grey world of the storm.

THE STORM KEPT PILING SNOW IN FRONT OF her. She was blinded. Even if she'd had a destination she wouldn't have been able to find it. All the instruments in the simple dash were spitting visual static at her. She watched them, trying to make sure she didn't turn around in the storm and head back.

For a brief while she had the lights of Base snug in her rear-view mirrors. But then the mirrors were frosted with snow and the lights were hidden by the storm.

She couldn't tell how far she'd come. She wasn't sure how far was enough. In the dark, the ice in front of her plough looked like all the other ice.

The only thing to do was to keep moving until the plough ran out of juice. There was no backup plan, no way to survive. She kept the hazard lights on as a warning to anyone passing, though she wasn't sure who was still alive.

The radio was quiet except for a low, static thrum. She wondered what had happened to Waterman. She wondered where Adriatico was.

Partly she wanted to lie down in the soft snow. She wanted to let the cold empty her out. To harden her and shatter her. She thought about Adriatico's belief in the soul. She wondered where her soul resided, if she had a soul. Was it the sternum, where she felt the greatest pain? Was it someplace where it could grow numb and tired the way the rest of her was numb and tired?

She figured it had to be a mechanism more primitive or more evolved than the heart or mind. A circuit all living things carried in their hands or torsos, waiting to be tripped. Waiting for something divine to activate it.

She pulled the mic around to her mouth. "If you can hear me, if anyone can hear me, get away, stay away from Base Station Un and—"

She clicked the mic off again before she was tempted to say too much. *Lock her out, don't let her in. Save your souls.* Who would believe it?

"SOS," she said out loud. "SOS."

When she realised someone had found her, she killed the lights and tried to wedge herself deeper into the cabin of the plough. *Not again*, she thought. *Not again.*

They dragged her out anyway. There was no stopping it.

"Tracked your SOS," said the stranger. "But honestly, mistook you for a runaway. Or a suicide."

He gestured at the weather outside the windshield of his supersized Seal and sent a look to Muir.

She wasn't sure he was wrong. She huddled into thin thermasheeting, shivering. Despite her best intentions, she was still trying to live.

Outside the window she caught sight of winter's first aurora borealis over the north. Streaks of green and brilliant yellow lit up the dark sky. She wished she could find it beautiful.

One pilot from the medivac flight just outside the atmosphere had broken rank, they told her. Taken an intra-atmosphere Seal, and dived to the planet surface in search of the distress beacons. To hear him tell it, he was a hero. Muir thought it more likely he was bored. A gung-ho cowboy looking to alleviate the blandness of all that dark space above the skin of the atmosphere. So far they hadn't spotted the mermaid's hand in the ice. Snow must have covered it.

Good, Muir thought. Her first coherent thought since he'd captured her.

"Can you believe they haven't even named this planet yet?" the pilot grumbled. "I mean, what's the holdup?"

He was clean-shaven, a foreign look after the months she'd spent on the ice. His face evenly toned and unburned. His hair was a deep bronze, curled around his temple.

"It defies them," Muir replied. "It's too... alien."

"Out here, aren't we the aliens?" The pilot chuckled.

Aren't we everywhere?

He offered her a cup of something hot but Muir couldn't hold it.

"I'm Murchadh," said the pilot, taking the cup back from her shaking hands. "Heard the distress signals. Ruptured walls, I'm guessing?"

"Okay." Muir nodded. It was the easiest thing to do.

Murchadh looked ex-army. He had the smooth, healthy look of someone that instinctively expected and inspired trust. His skin was pale, even for the eternal winter of space.

"We had one of those when I was on surface," he was saying. "Near miss. Don't build those things like they used to."

"You were on the surface?"

"At Deux. While ago, now."

Murchadh leaned back in his seat and looked to where Muir huddled beside him. She figured the next question would be a test.

"Before I take you up to the medivac ship, we should get to your Base. See what the others say. It means longer on the surface before we can get you up to a medic. That a problem?"

He watched Muir closely. She knew Murchadh suspected her of something worse than running.

"You think I'm crazy?" she asked.

"I didn't say that."

"You think I destroyed my own Base?"

Murchadh gave her a hard look. "Did you?"

She didn't take it personally. The ice did strange things to people. It brought out the animal.

"Sure, let's go check it out," she managed through chattering teeth. "There'll be others needing a medic, too."

She didn't add 'hopefully'. She wondered what had happened to Waterman, and whether the cold had come for Adriatico.

The storm was dying down outside. Murchadh lifted his Seal straight up, over the plough where he'd found Muir. She peered out at its fading lights. It looked like she'd driven the thing into a snow bank. The mermaid's hand was hidden.

Thank God, she thought.

Of the twenty-eight winter-overs at Base Station Un, only three remained when the rescue ship arrived.

They found Adriatico curled up in the pile of insulation jackets she'd crawled back to after opening the hangar doors. Her face was bruised black by frostbite, and she held her hands in front of her like claws. But her green eyes rolled round to fix on Muir when they carried her into the Seal, and there was the smallest smile on her face.

"You did it?" she asked in a husk of a voice.

"Yeah."

"You know each other?" Murchadh asked.

"Of course. That's Adriatico, Base doctor," Muir replied.

"Medici," Adriatico corrected her, voice breaking. "For the people who used to call me that."

Muir nodded. The nickname had made it out of Base Station Un, even if none of those who used it had.

They found Waterman, too, holed up in her Spryte, half-hanging over some unnamed precipice. The only other person they found was Partholon. He stank of something rotten. Something worse than rotten.

"Footman Muir," he sneered, eyes blank. "Muir the baby killer. Bringing death wherever she goes."

"How'd you survive, Partholon?"

"I prayed to the God of Ducks, little one," he said.

"Is that really what you saw in the ice, you son of a bitch?"

Partholon grinned, but then the grin faltered and something raw and uncontainable took its place.

"Friend of yours?" Murchadh shot her a sharp look.

"Him?" she spat. "Your friends ever call *you* baby killer?"

Murchadh was looking at her keenly. Not because he believed Partholon about the baby killing, she realised. But because he was wondering whether Partholon was worth saving.

"He's a scientist," she said. "He knows stuff about the ice."

It was as close as she could get to letting Partholon live.

After that, Partholon was silent a long time. The fight had gone out of him, and he wasn't the better for it. Muir found herself wanting to tell him about the sounds of their friends' bodies smashing against the frozen ground. About the silence.

"Where'd you go?" she asked.

"Dump truck," Partholon answered. "Hid in the back."

"With the rest of the garbage?" Muir asked.

"Touché," Partholon answered.

Waterman was holed up in a warm salt bath, where she screamed and screamed.

The others sat side by side, her and Partholon and Adriatico. They stared through the small porthole windows of Murchadh's Seal.

Space twinkled with icy blue-and-white stars, so densely packed that sometimes it looked like milk.

They shared cups of warm tea and didn't speak. Adriatico had bandaged her own face against the frostbite. White bandages that made her look blank. Muir figured Waterman might not make it.

Which meant Adriatico and Partholon were as close as she was going to get to people who understood what she'd been through. Not that she understood it herself.

Murchadh made them wait in the Seal while he scouted the remains of Base Station Un. Muir wanted to warn him that his extreme cold weather gear might not be extreme enough in that base, but Murchadh seemed so unaffected by the terror that gripped her, that eventually she subsided.

She cast a glance at Partholon, expecting ridicule. But Partholon's face was pinched with a similar fear. So she held her tongue and waited for Murchadh to return.

"Nothing else," Murchadh said when he got back. "No survivors apart from you four."

He'd become grim on that last trip, and the cowboy ease he'd displayed earlier had disappeared. Muir wanted to ask what he'd found, which particular part of the Base apocalypse was responsible for his new mood. But she didn't. Maybe it was all of it.

Murchadh lifted the large Seal into the air and skimmed low over the surface. The powerful lights caught on sharp angles of ice and snow as he built enough ignition to break the atmosphere and return to the medivac ship.

"Most of the wind's gone, at least," he commented from the pilot's chair. Then he made a 'huh' of surprise.

"What?" Muir asked.

Her skin prickled.

"The lights are on in your plough," Murchadh said.

"They should've burned out by now," Muir muttered.

She leaned into the small round window in front of her. Beside her, Partholon was uttering something in a language she didn't understand. From the cadences, she figured it for prayer.

She saw the lights and her stomach fell.

"Hell, no."

It wasn't until then that she realised she'd hoped to live through this.

"Oh, shit," said Adriatico in a voice muffled by bandages.

Partholon started to cry.

"Keep flying, Murchadh," Muir shouted. "Keep us in the air."

"But... what the hell is that?" Murchadh said, wonder softening his words.

And then it was too late all over again.

M URCHADH WOULDN'T LISTEN. NOT TO REASON, not to pleadings.

"At least take us to the medivac ship before you come back for her."

He twisted in his seat. "For who?"

Murchadh wanted to get the vision in the ice: the mermaid's hand, the ankh, the lotus petal. Or as he reported it, a serpent's head. Its mouth was open and its fangs sat wide in the block of ice.

Muir figured, at least this time the symbol was more honest. It was a thing sent to destroy. It had reached into their ancestral memories and found their triggers.

Moving to where Murchadh sat, Adriatico reached around him for the controls.

"If you don't get us to that ship," she said, voice muffled by bandages, "I'll crash this damn thing. Don't think for a second I won't."

Adriatico said later, Murchadh's eyes were blank and his pupils were narrow. But still he took them to the ship waiting just outside the atmosphere. And then he backed out of the hangar and headed down for the monster outside Base Station Un.

"Think we should tell the captain not to wait?" Partholon asked.

Waterman had been moved to a surgical room. They were operating on the blackened skin of her face and feet. They'd already made stumps of her hands.

"How do we explain it?" Muir asked.

Partholon hesitated. "We say, it's a virus."

"We didn't find anything alive down there. How could there be a virus?"

"They don't know that," Partholon whispered. "The records are all at Base."

"How long can a virus live in the ice?"

Partholon shrugged. "Frozen, maybe forever."

Muir's skin crawled. "Think they'll buy it?"

"I would."

But in the end, they waited for the inevitable. For Murchadh to return with the stars in his eyes.

On the medivac ship, they sat alone. No one wanted to get close to them. Not out of fear of viruses. Probably because of the strange, staring silences Muir found herself falling into. Partholon, too, she saw it in him. Adriatico was kept busy at Waterman's side. Trying to keep her alive, she explained, against her own failing heart and the defeatism of the medivac doctors.

"They're afraid of us," Muir commented.

"Yeah." Adriatico rolled her eyes.

Superstition festered in isolated places. Like ice, like space. Like the ocean village her mother had belonged to.

The medivac crew watched the survivors of Base Station Un with quick eyes. It was clear they wished they could have left them below, on the surface of the unnamed ice world. Muir would wish that, too, if she were them.

Someone delivered powdered eggs and cocoa at regular intervals, but it all tasted like grit to Muir. She ate automatically, out of some sense of duty.

Waterman was returned to them, what was left of her. They kept her sedated. Not for the frostbite but because of the gnawing sadness that filled her eyes whenever she was awake.

Muir cornered the ship's captain. A distinguished, greying man called Farraige.

"Why are we still here?" she asked.

"Is that an existential question?" Farraige responded, eyes clear and bright against his olive skin.

"We haven't moved. We're just hanging here."

"We're waiting for Murchadh to return."

"You think he'll do that anytime soon?"

Farraige eyed her. "And we're waiting for a freighter."

"Why..." She stopped. "You're going to load that thing into a freighter, aren't you? You're taking it home with you."

"Convoys are safer for travel," Farraige confirmed.

Not this one, Muir thought. "So it's going to be with us all the way back to Earth?"

There was a pulse going off in her neck. She rubbed at it, but she couldn't get it to settle.

"Are you collecting the bodies from Base?" she asked. "We should take them home. For..."

She was going to say 'burial', but she wasn't sure the icy ash could be buried.

"For funerals?" she said at last.

Farraige shook his head. "We don't have the capacity, I'm afraid."

"But you'll take a chunk of ice back, instead?"

"For study," Farraige nodded.

"Not for glory?"

Farraige muttered about his duties, how busy he was, he didn't have time. He asked her if she needed sedatives, whether a doctor could come see her.

"We have a doctor," she said.

She took the news of the freighter back to Partholon and Adriatico, but they barely reacted.

There was a new doctor leaning over Waterman. She gave her name as Mizu. Her hair was long and black, neatly gathered at her neck, and her eyes were bright green like the ocean.

"Can I get whatever you're giving her?" Partholon was asking.

Mizu looked like she was about to refuse, but then she glanced at Partholon's ravaged face.

"I'll get you something," she said.

"Me, too," Adriatico muttered. "What about you, Muir? Makes the time go."

"Go where?"

Nobody laughed. Muir took what the doctor offered: an innocuous white capsule.

Adriatico was right about the time. Muir welcomed the slowing down and thickening of her vision as the sedative took hold. She slumped gratefully into a bunk beside Adriatico and stared out into the milk of space.

The stars were being eclipsed by the spectre of the arrived freighter.

When the sedative wore off six hours later, she was sobbing.

By then the medivac ship was shifting across the bright emptiness of space, in perfect tandem with the freighter.

"Cried yourself out?" Adriatico asked.

"Doubt it." Muir rubbed at her face. "Plenty more where that came from."

The ocean of grief inside her ebbed, but it never evaporated. It barely washed the sides of the wide space inside her ribs.

Adriatico said, "Waterman's dead."

Adriatico told her how they'd found Waterman that morning, her eyes open, staring into the dark. She went on to describe everyone from Base Station Un, talking about their lives and deaths with equal calm.

Muir had been dreaming about them. In her dreams they were all still in the Base, still upright. In her dreams their whitened statues were made of salt, not ice. Sea salt. The kind that crusted her mother's clothes and the rattan baskets she carried for collecting the seaweed.

Her mother was never in the dreams, although Muir searched and searched for her.

"Headache?" Adriatico asked.

"Nah."

Muir had asked Mizu for something to end the dreams, but the medicines only made Muir numb. And somehow having those dreams clinging to the insides of her skull, ugly but unfrightening, felt worse with the meds in her system.

Muir said, "You know she will turn Earth to ice. Don't you? That's what she does. She'll destroy the whole place. Everything. Everyone."

"Maybe." Adriatico shrugged. "If we even make it that far."

Partholon said from his bunk, "The freighter's slowing down. Maybe she doesn't want us to get to Earth."

"She won't kill us out here," Muir said. "Not enough of a body count."

Partholon chuckled darkly. "What's a few people compared to a whole planet, right?"

"Right."

"What is she, your mermaid?" Partholon sat up and swung his legs over the bunk.

Muir didn't look at him. "She's not mine."

"But you've got the best connection to her," Partholon persisted. "When Base was going nuts over the stuff in the hangar, you were out there. You were with her."

Muir hesitated. "I don't know what she is."

"I'm not asking you for a full testable scientific theory," Partholon muttered. "I just want to know what you think, for chrissake."

"What I *think*?" Muir snapped. She took a breath and then let it out slowly. "I think she's the first Goddess. The very first. Bayoumi said she was the Goddess of War, but I think she's the Goddess of Everything. The Goddess of Goddesses."

The others were quiet, either mulling it over or figuring Muir for a crazy person, she didn't know which. She didn't care.

Partholon said, "Yeah, well, Bayoumi's dead. Everyone's dead."

"Yeah."

"Is it true that you killed a little girl?"

Muir started.

Adriatico said, "Shut up, Partholon. Not this again."

"Hey, a man's got a right to know."

"No, he doesn't," Adriatico muttered. "What's it even matter now?"

Muir thought it did matter, it had always mattered. But she couldn't find voice enough to say it.

Partholon rolled back into his bunk. "You know why Medici's

all the way out here with us, Muir? All the way out at the edges of space?"

"Shut up, Partholon, I mean it." Adriatico said. Her voice was nothing but tired.

"Or, what, you'll kill me?"

Muir glanced up as Partholon began to laugh in a weird, high voice. He was staring up at the ceiling. They hadn't looked each other in the eye for days, Muir realised. None of them had.

"Partholon, are you okay?" Muir asked.

"She made bombs," Partholon told the ceiling. "Isn't that right, Medici? You bombed someone."

"I was a kid," Adriatico said grimly. "I was stupid and I didn't think it through. And I hurt someone."

"Ah, never mind," Partholon said. "At least nobody died. For the young Medici, the conclusion was that you were some budding genius caught up in childhood hijinks."

"How do you know all that?" Muir asked.

"Court reports," Partholon supplied. "Marcella Adriatico. Psychologist's description was of a nine-year-old lacking in empathy."

Muir turned to Adriatico, but she wouldn't meet Muir's eye.

"Adriatico?"

"Like it was no big deal," Partholon continued. "A nine-year-old kid with no sense of fellow feeling. Isn't that weird?"

"No," Adriatico replied. "It's about normal for a nine-year-old."

"Well, that's even creepier," Partholon muttered. "Kids, hey?"

"How'd you even get your hands on court reports?" Muir asked.

Partholon made an exasperated noise deep in his throat, like it was easy. He rubbed the back of one hand across his dark, unshaven chin. "So they sent Medici here to live with the rest of us because she wasn't a good enough doctor to overcome a history of bombing kids."

"Partholon?" Adriatico said quietly. "You open your mouth around me again, I'm going to snap your spine."

She looked like she meant it.

Partholon grunted. "Hey, Muir?"

"What?"

"That little girl you killed? Probably wasn't your fault."

Muir gritted her teeth. "Thanks."

"As for you, Medici, you're only about as crazy as the rest of us."

They hadn't all been crazy. Waterman hadn't been crazy, not until the very end. Muir envied her. The ice had gotten to her, too, eventually. But until then, she'd kept hold of herself. Waterman had resisted giving herself to the grief.

Muir curled into her bunk and turned to face the wall.

"You tired, Muir?" Adriatico asked.

"Always."

"Yeah. Me, too."

From then on, Muir's dreams were all of the mermaid.

The medivac ship had slowed to a crawl. The metal insides rumbled with engine thrust that had been thwarted by some other force, out in the distance of space.

Muir sought out Captain Farraige in his rooms.

"She's holding us back," Muir began.

"She?" Farraige smiled kindly

"The mermaid." *He thinks I'm mad*, Muir realised. "We're being pulled backwards, aren't we?"

"We have a problem with our acceleration—"

"It's the freighter," Muir interrupted. "Correction, what's on the freighter. If you don't believe me, try using the accelerators to go backwards. I bet it works."

Farraige frowned. "You talk as if this thing in the ice has a mind of its own."

Muir was quiet. She wasn't sure if that was entirely right. She thought perhaps the mermaid fed on the minds she found, and the wills of the people she gathered to her.

Right now, the skeleton crew of Farraige's ship must be feeling it, that possessive desire to keep the mermaid for themselves, to keep it quiet and not share it with the world. Perhaps only Farraige's appetite for glory was keeping them moving at all.

Muir said, "She wants to go back to her world. You should let her."

"We'll push through," Farraige replied.

Muir looked at him. She said softly, "You will, won't you? You're just not going to stop."

"Of course not. We can't go back now."

"You can."

"Please! If we reverse now," Farraige reflected, like he was considering some philosophical question, "we'll collide with the freighter."

"I don't mean it literally," Muir muttered. "You could circle around. In fact, wait, you should just dump her here. Clear out the personnel from the freighter, bring them on this ship. Then just let her drift. She'd hate that."

Farraige chuckled. "Would she?"

He made the slightest change to his posture, but it took him from relaxed to alert. Muir sensed it more than saw it. He thought she was a dangerous madwoman.

She straightened and watched Farraige size her up. She felt a flash of warm rage.

That's when it dawned on her. She liked the idea of getting the mermaid home and forcing Earth to freeze. She wanted it to freeze. She wanted the whole planet, the whole, messed-up place to be frozen where it sat. Icicles like crystals in every tree and eave. Streets paved with slippery ice, water smoothed over and stilled. Every window rimed with ice. Frost across all the buildings and street signs and faces of every single person.

All life, all anger, all suffering and history, all gone. None of this fighting for survival. No one left to hear the crack and crunch of ice as it moved relentlessly across the world's surface. All humanity swallowed and the world a soft, white, blank slate.

She felt the ice in her own heart then. She curled herself around it.

"You know why they sent me out here?" she asked.

Farraige shrugged. "You were a pilot, so I'm told."

"A pilot, sure, but that's not why they chose me," she said. "It was part of my sentence."

Farraige recoiled, ever so slightly. So he hadn't known this bit. They must've sealed her records after all. That's why Partholon kept asking. Not because he wanted her to admit what she'd done. But because he didn't know.

"I got twenty years for what I did, but with this stinking job, I was going to be out in twelve. Then I could go wherever I wanted. I was going to be free."

Farraige smiled noncommittally.

"The people I worked with, they knew I'd done something. They knew I killed someone. A girl. They worked it out somehow. Probably pieced that much together from news reports, I don't know." She smiled. "I'm rambling."

"Not at all," Farraige said.

"See, I drove freighter trucks. My speciality was the Northwest Quadrant back on Earth."

"That's a bad spot. Can get pretty risky in bad weather," Farraige replied.

"Yeah."

"Takes a capable driver."

Muir looked out the tiny portholes at the darkness, imagining the swirls of life that lived inside it. Surrounded by it. "It does, doesn't it?"

"So, whatever you did, Ms Muir—"

"This day, this particular day, they gave me equipment to deliver. It was a test, I guess. Scientific equipment. All kinds of glass, like test tubes and beakers and hell, I don't even know. It was all on the manifest, but I didn't need to read much of that to know what I was carrying was fragile." She paused and closed her eyes. "The drive was going to take a couple of days, so I started straight away. Wanted to get it done before ice closed the roads. I drove all day and all night and into the next day. I was most of the way there by then."

Farraige shifted in his seat, but he didn't speak. He was listening, she realised. This time, he was listening.

"It was still dark, and I'd been up for twenty-four hours or so. Stopping for petrol and not much else. I drove straight through, running the roads. And before that, I'd been on a week-long drive. Same sort of thing. Hardly any sleep. Just me and the roads, me and the crackle of the radio. Man. The shit people say when they think they're anonymous, right? I just can't stand…" She laughed, catching sight of Farraige's confused expression. "People. I can't really stand people."

Farraige relaxed. "I think you're tired right now. Perhaps you need to return to your bunk."

"I am," Muir admitted. "I am tired. But this is a different kind of tired to back then. There was this little girl. She was out there on the road, and she was just… standing there. You know?"

"She was lost?"

"Who the hell knows? Found out later she was the daughter of one of the scientists up there. She'd just moved up there because her mother had died..."

Muir's voice trailed off. Farraige rested his hands one on top of the other.

"That's..." he began. He didn't finish whatever he'd been going to say. He didn't seem to know how.

"She was just standing there. I didn't see her until really late. It was snowing, you know?"

Muir frowned, trying to remember it. The dreams of the mermaid kept getting in her way, icing up her memories so they didn't run so good.

"I mean, I'm paid for speed, right?" she continued. "I'm paid for the fastest delivery. And the least amount of breakage. But all that stuff wobbling in the back of the truck, wrapped in paper or whatever the hell they thought would keep it safe. Cocooned. Supposed to be kept safe. But mostly, I'm paid for speed."

"Right."

"So as soon as I saw her there, in the middle of the damn road, I knew my bonus was gone. I was going to have to slow down or swerve or whatever-the-hell. Any of that, at those speeds, was going to cause me issues on the iced-up roads. I slow, the load might fishtail, the whole cargo container might swing around towards me, might even snap. I swerve, I probably slide the whole thing off the road, me with it. Do you believe that?"

"I've never driven freighters. But sure, I can see that. A large vehicle, at speed. On ice. Hard to control."

"Right, that's it." Muir nodded. "They just pretty much skid forward over most of those roads. Don't even need a driver some of the time. We're just there in case... well. In case of the worst, I guess. Whatever happened, I was never going to make that deadline, not after that little girl appeared."

Muir paused to clear her throat.

Farraige said quietly, "So, what did you do?"

"Thing was, I'd seen her too late."

"Because of the snow."

"Right," Muir agreed. "Because of the snow."

"You probably didn't have the time—"

"I had time," Muir snapped.

"For what?" Farraige asked easily. "Those trucks are just large, clumsy weapons, Ms Muir. One of you was in for it."

"Yeah," Muir agreed. "But there's always time for a different decision, you notice that? I'd lost my delivery bonus and I'd be out of pocket for whatever damn glass tubes I broke. And maybe I'd have to pay damages on the truck. At that speed, if I tried to change course the drivetrain might seize up or the wheels might lock. Frame might even snap, who knows what the cold would've done to it."

Farraige shrugged. "Maybe. I'm no mechanic."

"Me, either. It's not like there was a mechanic anywhere near that neck of the woods. Just a bunch of damn idiot scientists needing their damn tubes. If the truck is damaged in the middle of nowhere, you're on your own. You're dragging your freight along the road on your damn hands and knees or something, I don't know."

Farraige smiled sadly.

The ice, the truck, the glass, the little girl. It was a calculation Muir had made over and over, but she'd never come up with a different result.

"Not your fault," Farraige said.

Muir chuckled drily. She was beginning to sound like Partholon. "Not how it works. Nobody cares about fault. Only delivery."

Part of her wondered whether the mermaid had been sent just for her, just for this. To punish her by destroying everyone she'd ever known.

Let Earth die, she thought. *Let her goddamn die.*

"So," she said, "I didn't swerve."

Farraige looked at her.

"I kept going straight. Took my foot off the accelerator, but didn't touch the brake. Too dangerous."

Muir looked at him. He was staring at her silently.

"I don't think the girl expected that. I figure she saw the truck coming, and maybe she liked to play chicken. But I guess she'd always won until then."

"She didn't move at all?"

"She moved finally. But too slowly. She took off to one side of the road, but those freighters are wide. They're wide and they're fast and those ones I was driving, they have those great, big snow scrapers on the front. Like a monstrous arrowhead. You know the type."

Farraige nodded.

"I made a decision, is all. I decided to let her die. No, not let her die. Make her die. So I could get the tubes to the damn scientists. So I could have my bonus."

"You were exhausted. You weren't thinking right."

"I don't know, captain. That moment when I made the decision, I felt wide awake. Like I'd never been more awake."

"It was the panic," Farraige told her. "The adrenalin."

"Maybe."

"You were in a dangerous position, with the freighter."

Muir shrugged. "I didn't even feel the impact. Heard it, though. Wasn't very loud. She didn't have to die like that."

"I'm sorry, Muir."

"They called it manslaughter. Voluntary manslaughter. So they locked me up for a while. Then they sent me way out here."

Farraige was silent.

"I took the offer, because... I was just trying to live, you see? That was my mistake. I thought I'd be able to live."

The room was quiet a long time. Muir felt like she was trying to imprint every detail of the room onto her retinas. Farraige, in his chair. The ship's controls splayed around him like winking eyes. The windows letting the blackness leak in. Muir moved towards them, rounding Farraige's chair.

"Yep, that was one decision," she said softly. "And this is another."

She reached out and gripped Farraige by the back of his neck. She moved fast, because speed was her ally, not strength.

She managed to unbalance him from his chair and as he fell, she drove an elbow into his spine just above and between his shoulder blades. She heard something snap. It sounded like the crunch of ice beneath a boot, or the shift of a truck's gears as it picked up speed.

It was quick. Blood poured from Farraige's mouth onto the floor. She tried to let him down gently, but he was too heavy for her. He fell and she dropped with him, rolling him off her trapped arm.

Then she was up and securing the doors.

After that, she passed to the controls. One thing Muir had always possessed was an understanding of engines. She found the levers and pulled on them, throttling the engines all the way back.

From around the ship, the alarms began to sound. She could hear shouting on the intercom, but the only voice she listened to was Partholon's as he laughed that familiar, cruel laugh. She muted all the other channels until it was only him, then she flipped through the vid-channels.

"Muir the baby killer." Partholon was grinning up at the vid-screen. "What in hell have you gone and done?"

"I may have found a way to save the world," she said.

Beside Partholon, Adriatico was unwrapping her scorched face. "So. Is that what you're going to do?"

"Yeah, baby killer, what're you thinking of doing?"

She hesitated. "I'm not sure."

She looked at her colleagues, but she could find nothing in their gazes.

"Well, decide quick, little Muir," Partholon said. "They'll be coming for you."

She couldn't move.

"Muir?" Adriatico said.

She said, "What do you think, Medici?"

Adriatico took a patient breath. "Think through the options. We can take this thing back to Earth and let it destroy the entire planet. Or, we can let Earth live, oblivious to the payload we're dragging."

"The mother load of payloads," Partholon shouted. "Up to you, baby killer."

Adriatico was steadier. "Whatever you think fair, Muir. Your decision."

"Why me? You guys aren't going to help me?" Hot tears burned her eyes.

"With you all the way, Muir," Partholon said. "Either way, we're dead, girl."

For once, his voice was soft. He'd lost that raucous timbre at last. Muir felt like she almost missed it.

"Either way," Muir repeated.

Adriatico nodded. Her leaden face was unreadable.

"Partholon?" Muir said.

"Yeah?"

"Tell me one thing. What'd you see in the ice, you freak?"

"Worst thing I ever saw, Muir."

"Was it the Devil?"

"If it was the Devil, baby girl, then shit!" His smile faltered. "The Devil has my face."

They were quiet. She saw Adriatico grip Partholon's hand. With her other hand, she made the Sign of the Cross from forehead to chest and both shoulders.

"Ah, hell," Muir said. Then again, "Ah, hell. Got to die sometime."

She gunned the medivac in flight, full throttle reverse into the freighter's hull, shoving it backwards along its path. She felt the tearing of metal around her and the rush of emptiness that came with distant space crowding in, crushing her.

And even then she couldn't tell if she was saving the world or not. But she knew that sometimes the cruellest thing wasn't to let the world die. It was to *force* the world to live.

In all its tragedy and grief and failure, it had to live.